The Virtuoso

D0949172

Margriet de Moor

The Virtuoso

Translated from the Dutch by Ina Rilke

THE OVERLOOK PRESS

WOODSTOCK & NEW YORK

First published in paperback in the United States in 2002 by
The Overlook Press, Peter Mayer Publishers, Inc.
Woodstock & New York

Woodstock:
One Overlook Drive
Woodstock, NY 12498
www.overlookpress.com
[for individual orders, bulk and special sales, contact our Woodstock office]

New York:
141 Wooster Street
New York, NY 10012

Library of Congress Cataloging-in-Publication Data

Moor, Margriet de.
[Virtuoos. English]
The virtuoso / Margriet de Moor ; translated from the Dutch by Ina Rilke.
p.   cm.
I. Rilke, Ina. II. Title.
PT5881.23.O578V5713   2000   839.3'1364—dc21   99-086847

Published by arrangement with Macmillan Publishers Ltd.

Manufactured in the United States of America

1 3 5 7 9 8 6 4 2
ISBN 1-58567-003-0 (hc)
ISBN 1-58567-253-X (pbk)

The Virtuoso

PROLOGUE

One day a boy vanished from our village. Gasparo Conti
had a pale, childish face, he was plump but as lithe as a
tufted reed, and when he ran barefoot in the backstreets
of the village brandishing a forked twig, his voice, his
shouts, sounded just as shrill as those of any boy in
Campano. His white shirt, his breeches: clothes that
would be handed down to uncomplaining brothers or
cousins. His gold-flecked eyes. He vanished, aged eleven,
after his father and mine had spent the whole night at
the card table.

The name of the village is Croce del Carmine and we
lived on the outskirts towards the west. The villa had
two floors and on the roof there was a turret. A stepped
terrace led down on three sides to a yard with cypress
and wild peach trees. At one time this place must have
radiated luxury and refined taste, but in my memory I
see shuttered windows, a closed harpsichord, and I can
hear the wind in the bundles of twigs that lay piled up

under the arcades of the outbuilding during winter. And of course I remember the room facing west where my father and Benedetto Conti played cards. It was July. The windows were open. The air wafting into the room on that becalmed day must inevitably have contained traces of smoke from the volcano. His features drawn and pale, Benedetto Conti waited for the stake that would enable this whole night to be effaced at one stroke.

'. . . Gasparo's operation.'

And the following Sunday my father stayed at home and it was Faustina, the nursemaid, who took me to the Santa Monica. By the time we reached the nave the *Gloria* had already been sung. A knot of women stepped aside to let us pass. Faustina pushed me into a pew, bent over me and, with a rapid gesture, she smoothed my new dress with the big golden birds. I looked at the choir. Four boys dressed in red were descending the altar steps on the right of the organ to sing, in a pool of light, a four-part motet. I knew them all.

Gasparo, the lead soprano, had been replaced.

I felt no emotion at first. Listening with all the expert knowledge of my ten years, I was not immediately able to identify the composition with the measured organ accompaniment. Certain upper partials seemed to be missing. The four voices sang with youthful ardour and the maestro made it quite clear that he would conduct his *Laudate* skywards single-handed if necessary. But I was reminded of a day in the autumn, dull and overcast, when there is no contrast of light and shade. Then, suddenly, I was filled with an unknown grief, and an apprehension as if something had splintered in my chest. As I bowed my head I realized my father had known the mass would not be worth his while this Sunday.

'I want you to tell me where Gasparo has gone,' I said as we made our way to the portal.

Faustina reached out to touch the water and crossed herself. Then she said: 'He's probably ill.' But I continued to look at her, refusing to budge, so that she was obliged to add: 'I've heard that he is in Norcia.' Then her voice dropped and she began to tell me about Norcia being the birthplace of St Benedict, an abbot who was so superhumanly pious that he did not die an ordinary death lying in bed but standing on his own two feet, his eyes fixed on the Madonna. I listened, knowing that she was misleading me, but her soft voice made my attention wander. I laid my hand in hers and meekly allowed myself to be led home. Norcia, I thought drowsily now and then, and that was all.

Yet, afterwards, the name of that place continued to ring in my ears like a mysterious and disturbing refrain. And years later it did not surprise me to hear of the operations that are skilfully performed there, in Norcia.

The boy must not be older than twelve years of age, twelve is the limit, but long before that the boy destined for song must be kept under scrutiny. Only an expert can tell when the change sets in from rounded cheek to angular jaw. There is a glimmer of fatigue in the eyes that betrays the tentative searching of skin and blood. This is the turning-point. Lips and cheeks are still those of a child, but there is an awkwardness of limb that tips the balance: tomorrow the horses will be harnessed. The surgical intervention in Norcia is not particularly taxing. Only one boy in four fails to survive. The surgeon sets out to remove seminal ducts and testicles without damaging any further tissues. If the undertaking is successful – and this is often enough the case – the child will regain both his physical strength and all his spirit once the wound has healed. He will grow and develop, and the glands that have been left to him will, thanks to the exceptional circumstances, provide his organism with a variety of original, innocent, scintillating accents. A skin that is soft and virtually hairless. A rib-cage with plenty of room for well-exercised lungs. And a larynx, perfectly modelled, which produces a voice of heart-rending beauty, a voice which moves, captivates, which attests to a world beyond this world but which comes none the less from a body like every other: warm, full of obscure desires.

*

The summer months went by. August, being the time between two harvests, found the villagers at the foot of Vesuvius in a celebratory mood. At daybreak I was often wonderfully roused by the sound of farm wagons going past our house on their way back to the village. Voices had been singing and violins and calcedons playing since the company's departure the day before. I love the early-morning hours. The new day creeps in at the window and tweaks you by the nose.

One evening my father took me to the square to hear a troupe of musicians from Naples. It was the name-day of St Bibiana. The village was full of chaises and carts. I remember that my father already had great difficulty walking, yet he ignored the grandstand seats on the platform under the canopy. From the midst of the crowd we watched and listened to the music, which was so tempestuous that it resembled rage. Neapolitans cannot abide slow tempi. Two violins, two mandolins and a cello accompanied a male and a female singer thrusting their canzonetta ever higher by means of the most curious tonal convolutions. Both voices were sopranos. When the girl happened to be singing the underlying melody, her partner, the *musico*, continued to produce his frenetic trebles with the utmost ease. All around me people clapped and shouted, couples danced, there was a smell of fire in the night air. When the song was over there was some discussion among the audience. I heard my father say: 'Very tolerable on the ear.' His voice sounded affable. I thought he would invite the whole group to come to our house, as he had done on other occasions.

But the following morning I stood in the doorway of the kitchen and saw that the ovens were cold. The servants wandered around aimlessly. And the only instrument to be tuned that day was the small cedar-wood keyboard on which I practised my Scarlatti sonatas.

Was I supposed to share my father's nostalgia, as well as his exile?

I wished I were in a ballroom with someone telling me a brand-new secret. I wished my sister would come home to visit.

She came. One beautiful Saturday a *carozza* drawn by six horses rattled into the drive with two smiling women under the half-raised hood: Angelica Margherita, my father's eldest daughter, and her aunt. For the first instant I was blinded. Then I looked into my sister's face. A grown lady, all of seventeen years, she was sitting on her haunches before me, she had kissed me, taken me in her arms and now demanded, her eyes anxiously flitting this way and that, to know at once whether I was laughing, eating, sleeping enough. She was stunning. Crowning her curly hair she wore a sugarloaf-shaped hat with cock feathers like any old wine merchant's.

Angelica Margherita, my half-sister, was seven years my senior. Her entire youth had been spent in preparation for a strategic marriage. She herself had different ideas. One Palm Sunday, encouraged by the absence of a mother and the absent-mindedness of her father, she set out for Naples to visit a young aunt who had made beauty and pleasure the principles of her life. After a year my father understood that he could save himself the expense of a dowry.

The house flew into an uproar. From the cellar to the attic the air was filled with shouted instructions to open cupboards and fill decanters. In the dining-room my father sat listening to his daughter's news.

She was learning Greek. She conversed on the subject of electricity. She possessed five French gowns.

The aunt leaned forward. 'Since spring she's been a ballerina, dancing in the Bartolomeo Theatre.'

In the mirror I could see my father's incredulous smile.

But it was true. Late at night, when we went to bed, my sister explained to me how a woman can defy the Pope and dance on stage for all to see, not only in Naples, but also in Rome. It was childishly simple: one dresses up as who one is. Somewhere along that whole row of young dancers, whose shaved cheeks, make-up and frocks exude such exotic femininity, there is always a girl. She wears the same wig as the boys and the same dancing frock over the regulation thigh-hugging pants. Yet she may by her sheer presence be the very one to bring about the so ardently desired equivocation, the dizziness.

Angelica Margherita removed her bodice as if she

were untying a blindfold. From my bed I watched the quivering subside from her breasts: soft, nacreous pink.

She said: 'It's such fun there. Believe me, honestly, one is driven mad with joy.'

Days of splendour followed. Driving around the countryside with the two women on our way to visit relatives, I would lean back and my gaze would rise from the horses up to the sky, and in no way was I different from a big, exhilarated butterfly.

Yes, but one time I heard my sister muttering: 'Go to the devil.' She was standing among the cypresses in the courtyard. It was almost dusk. She was staring at the house and the stepped terrace and the shutters like someone who has the evil eye. A day later she said: 'It's not much fun here in winter.'

Soon after that she left again, with her companion, to go and dance on a stage hung with velvet draperies, against a dreamlike backdrop of domes and galleries which vanish into distance and transform the face of the world.

And I stayed behind in a deserted village.

*

I must say that I come from a pretty village. All the houses, large and small, have courtyards with flowers and birds. And on a paved square in the centre stands a church with a brightly painted organ which is known as the Divina Pietà. The village lives off the sun and the

Vesuvius-drenched soil, which is far from poor. Grapes, corn and fruit thrive in the sulphurous fumes that rise from holes in the ground at the oddest moments. Above the buildings shimmers the sky and under the sky, in the distance, the volcano is smoking. That lovely village was my father's place of exile. I was born in a place of exile.

When my father left for Spain on a big grey horse at the beginning of the century to go and fight for Philip, he was by no means alone. The Neapolitan noblemen supported the kings of Castile and Aragon. My father set out at the head of a hundred well-trained troops, at his own expense, to defend Catalonia and the kingdom of Naples against the Habsburgs. How he came to regret his honourable endeavour! He returned to his native town after a year of fire and blood to find the eagle standard flying on the roof of the royal palace: Charles of Habsburg had seized Naples. The Austrian was in a forgiving frame of mind. My father and several other barons were banished to their country estates.

The villa saw good times, initially, and the local population earned good extra money. I know that my father and his second wife, my mother, gave spectacular parties. Angelica Margherita remembers the masks and the costumes woven with gold thread. I don't remember that kind of thing. I was only three years old when, just before the siesta hour, my mother collapsed with a sigh on the pink marble floor of her bedroom. Faustina, who was with her, described how the tortoise-shell combs she had just pulled from her black hair simply dropped from her hands. Was that the moment when the soul departed from the house? My father must have resigned himself little by little, since that day of death, to the emptiness of exile. And more than ever before he must have sought refuge in the only thing left to the stranger in this life. Oblivion. Cards, drunkenness, love, music: blissful moments in a world that is not one's own. My father's indulgences were dice and cards.

How often, when the sun had set, didn't I hear the friends, the practised players, entering our house and making their way to the room facing west? I knew the sounds of the thirty-and-forty game, of the *banco fallito*, and I knew the silence interrupted by soft-spoken expletives when, some evenings, *minchiate* was played. Ninety-seven large playing-cards with designs by Michelangelo are quickly shuffled and dealt. The stakes are high. Each debtor keeps track of his losses on the white back of a card. My father lost his money and his fields, his carriages, his horses, his Portuguese coins. And he had one opponent whom he – the Holy Virgin only knows why – was unable to resist.

There comes Benedetto Conti, one night in July, I see him on the terrace steps in front of the house. Behind the doors in the hall my father is waiting to welcome him. The two men shake hands and look at each other with vacant eyes. Both are on their guard. It is with great reserve that they seek each other out for the purpose of succumbing to a high-handed, strictly personal adventure. In the scorched air coming in through the windows they take their seats at the table and begin to drink and play poker. They stay sober like demons in hell. Two, three hours go by, Conti is losing. Even when they have switched to playing cards Conti continues to lose corn, wine, land, and his face grows pale. Then he raises his eyes. My father does the same. Their eyes meet.

Was that when my father, inspired by the unanticipated turn his fortunes were taking, began to think of the other things he valued in life? Suddenly there was a small matter that urgently needed to be settled with Conti.

'All right,' he said softly. 'Let's see if we can reverse this situation by means of one simple stake.' He smiled and pulled a patient face.

The voice of Gasparo. The voice of Gasparo Conti, that incredible entity directing the choirs of singers and ensembles of musicians in the entire region, had already preoccupied my father's thoughts for some time. He and other insiders had drawn Conti's attention to the future awaiting the boy: riches and adulation. But the man gave an impression of utter indifference, indeed, of it not being any concern of his. Assistance in running his vineyards was provided by his eldest sons, which left the youngest, the prodigy, to grow up without let or hindrance. Rome ... Naples ... the opera houses all over Europe ... Conti would yawn or whistle between his teeth. Only at night, at the green-baize table, did he display his firm conviction that he was born to win.

'Gasparo's operation.'

Conti nodded and laid out his cards one by one, holding them between thumb and forefinger. He lost.

He lost and there was nothing to stop the boy from disappearing from our village. At first I didn't know where I got the idea that Gasparo had taken something away from me, something I wanted to keep at all cost. After that my thoughts would often wander, and a radiant childhood hour flashed across my memory. He was eleven and I was ten. He was standing before the curved church wall, I was sitting at the corner of the first pew. The light pouring in through the windows converged in the centre of the space. For a moment it was completely still. Then, at a sign from the choir-master, the aria began. In antiphony with the choir Gasparo sang an air I had never heard before. Astonished, I followed the soft opening bars, the protracted tone, to a crescendo that stretched taut like a cord of silk. What was happening? Was the vault in the church too narrow? I sat upright and looked at the singing boy. It was as if I knew that I had to impress his contented red lips on my memory for years ahead, his brow, his hair, his surplice with the lace sleeves, and the throat with which he, showing no emotion at all, emitted a stream of sounds that carried me with them in their flow ... Affection. Trust. Links between two domains. It was not until the choir fell in for the last time that I finally understood my predicament. I shut my eyes tightly and thought: Oh, what turbulence! What longing! I am happy.

Was that love, then, already?

Many years later I set eyes on him again. A tall man with rounded shoulders. In his youth he had travelled to Norcia unaware that he, in the semi-darkness of his carriage, was taking with him the fancy of a young girl.

*

When I reached the age of fifteen it was time to marry. In our region the women reach the peak of their beauty at that age, never in their lives will they be more beautiful. I was an aristocrat with raven-black hair, which was plaited by my chambermaid Faustina and folded into a green silk snood just so that it would hang exactly above my shoulders. I had a wasp waist, a strong nose, and unflinching eyes under brows extending to my temples.

That I had been taught Latin and heraldry was nothing unusual. That I should be invited to the grand houses in the region was to be expected. Young women like me presented ourselves in low-cut dresses of flowered brocade. We sang. We improvised on the harpsichord. After a supper of wild boar with honey, pigeon, lamb, hare, sea bass in hot red sauce, risotto, sorbet, chocolate, cake and the first cherries from orchards irrigated with warm water, we would be entreated to recite poems about gods and shepherdesses out in the open air, among the dwarf palms on the terrace. And we would comply with astonishing ease.

But my dowry had gradually dwindled to nothing.

One day my father said: 'The Duke of Rocca d'Evandro has asked for your hand in marriage.'

I burst out laughing. 'Berto?'

My father did not bat an eyelid.

Berto, the man who wanted me for his wife, was a friend of the family whom I had known since childhood. He came from a family of lawyers whose resources were bottomless thanks to the disposition of Neapolitans to rekindle old feuds with relatives or neighbours from one moment to the next, and to fight them out in the courts, if need be from generation to generation. The judiciary of Naples with all her princes and barons is wider-ranging than the parliament in Paris. Berto owned farms and estates, carriages and horses and a palace on the via Toledo. His ducal title had been purchased. At the time of his proposal of marriage he was already past forty. I knew him as a man with inquiring jet-black eyes which could see straight through me as if there were someone else standing behind my person.

As to my person, there were two conditions my betrothed demanded of me. I was to live on his estate near Altavilla, some forty miles away, and not in his house in Naples. I would not, in his presence, perfume myself with either amber or musk. We married on a merciless winter day.

Never will I be heard to denigrate the state of marriage. Suddenly I was living in a luxurious and orderly home, where my friends, my father and my sister came to visit me. I installed Faustina in the cabinet adjoining my bedroom with its pleasing frescos. I ordered my servants around, and was just as happy to invite them into the salon on occasion, for among them were four excellent musicians: two guitarists, a cellist and a violinist. It was especially with the latter, my husband's manservant, that I experienced wonderful hours of inspiration. We played the Thuringian Bach, the Venetian Vivaldi, and when we played all Corelli's violin sonatas we took the licence of concluding a piece in a minor key with a minor third, just for fun – and why not? Whenever the youth started playing Besozzi's wonderful solo, Berto was sure to turn up. He would listen thoughtfully to the performance by the young man wearing white trousers. I was accustomed to the two of them disappearing to Naples at the most unexpected moments.

We got along well together, Berto and I. That he was often away for months on end did not bother me, it was part of our contract. But when he sat behind the candlestick at the head of the table, conversing left and right with our guests, I would view him with fondness. It wasn't bad at all living with this trusted companion in the same house, and sometimes, in the hottest hours of the day, to lie in the same bed. The anatomy of his body, the mechanics of it, had not disappointed my curiosity. His big soft hands and the things he said in the dark soon made my thoughts wander. I didn't find it in the least troubling that he seemed to be aware of my yearning. So this was love. I became enamoured of that tyranny of panic and bliss. The afterglow too I enjoyed, the languor as if you had lain with your legs in the sun.

'You aren't getting impatient, are you?' I asked my husband one summer night.

For the object of it all was of course that my husband's name and estate should be carried on for posterity. When I bore Berto a daughter at the beginning of the second year of our marriage, his reaction was gallant. He took the infant in his arms and laughed at the tiny yawning mouth. Three years later a second girl was born. Again there was much endearment, and fireworks over the orange trees. No, he was not impatient. Berto brought my emerald-ringed fingers to his lips and vanished for more than eight months to the Catholic city overlooking the heathen bay.

Churches ... processions in the streets ... purple sails blowing into port ... Naples beckoned. My sister's descriptions of the damask cloths festooning the houses did not make me happy, I just turned away. 'That city embraces all of you,' said Angelica Margherita. 'You sleep in it, and you walk, ride, dance in it. Yet you never know for sure what's going on.' My gaze dissolved into the golden landscape outside my window and church bells started ringing of their own accord and statues of saints speaking softly, by turns in Spanish and Neapolitan. I really must go there, I thought. But I did nothing, not for a long time. Without knowing why, I simply waited. My restlessness and my indecision did not change until the ban proclaimed against my father was lifted.

For one day the Spaniards returned to Naples. While the dynasties of Europe were entangled in a new war of succession, Charles of Bourbon, son of the Spanish king, had marched into the city at the head of his army. The short, good-natured prince, whose luggage contained a celebrated collection of paintings, dispatched the Habsburgs and ascended the throne. Naples applauded. After almost three centuries the Kingdom of Two Sicilies had a royal court of its own once more. What would my father do now? Would he return to that exhilarating place? Surely he would?

My father fell ill. The triumph in his eyes faded rapidly. At first he said he would bide his time because his return, naturally, would have to be properly prepared. Then he grumbled that the winter was lasting very long. He said he did not wish to eat. I persuaded him to lodge with me and summoned various physicians.

Each evening I sent the two guitarists to his bedside to play for him. We tried to cheer him up. Faustina rubbed his legs with oil and rue. Berto spoke of the opera house that the king was having built in Naples, an oval fantasy six storeys high with scores of blue velvet boxes and balustrades fitted with candle-lit mirrors, so that the symmetry of the space, which was devised to suspend all sense of time and proportion, was carried to alarming extremes ... My father listened with a tranquil smile but one day he said that he would no longer take drink. I think his dying was flight.

Not long after that I undertook the journey. In the half-light of an early morning I took my seat beside Berto in one of his smartest green carriages and turned to look at the house. In a moment I would wave at my two daughters and their nurses until we were out of sight. A whip cracked. Were we ready? Had we forgotten nothing? I crossed myself, Berto smiled at me, we had come to an amicable agreement. After I had spent a full season in Naples, I would return home and would become pregnant again. With the Madonna's blessing I would bear a son. The morning air caressed my cheek. We left with three carriages: besides Faustina I was taking a load of wigs and dresses with me.

Cypresses, vineyards, the sky paled. The red ploughed earth was spotted with dark birds and a dog lay asleep at the foot of a boulder. Thinking back on that journey I know I saw the landscape as a stage-set. Something was about to happen. No ordinary event, no banality calmly waiting its turn in the passage of time, but something artful and premeditated. Once I believed that past and future are separate things. They are not. There are no stories without quotations. Events step from one time-span into the other. As I watched a flock of goats scrambling down a hillside I sighed deeply, I felt a rush of excitement I had felt before.

Of course I did not think of Gasparo.

But long before reaching the coast the traveller can sense the sea.

I

I'll talk to him. I'll take my glass and go up to him, and engage in the kind of polite conversation no one in their right mind can be bothered with. Not that I lack inspiration. I am a force field of inspiration. The fever, which will no doubt persist for a while, arose a few hours ago, in the San Carlo theatre, at the very moment I first heard him sing here in Naples. Sitting between my husband and my sister in a box on the second tier I listened to a male voice that transcended everything I have ever known and understood. I was overwhelmed, the world around me started to float. This is the beginning, but of what?

I stroll across the salon in his direction, avoiding trousers and skirts; I bump into a crystal table, I catch my reflection in a green-tinted mirror, a strange gleam in my eyes. When there is no more than a yard separating his body from mine I speak out, loud and clear: 'Sir, your singing was truly splendid!'

He barely turns away from the people milling around him. There is no change in the faintly smiling expression as his eyes veer towards me, I stand still and look. Tall, a tall figure. Sturdy, a puff-sleeved jacket strains across his chest. Swollen, his lips are just as girlish and plump as I remember them from long ago.

Holy Virgin. God. How can I make him see the gravity of the situation?

'Your arias were infinitely more vivacious than those of la Stradina.'

Now it seems to dawn on him that I might have a great, extraordinary secret to divulge. Turning his back on his companions he smiles at me.

'La Stradina is a whining bitch,' he says.

I nod, speechless.

'And her sixteenth passages are simply gruesome.'

Gold-flecked eyes. Soft pristine cheeks. And a speaking voice as monotonous as a shower on a windless day.

'. . . That a shake can be pleasing in two different ways is obvious to every fool. But in one and the same passage, for goodness' sake, make up your mind: it's got to be either the goat trill or the *gruppo*. Personally I have nothing against the *gruppo*. You can alternate smoothly and rapidly with the second above and keep the other sixteenths distinct like the drops of a fountain. But the really hard work is of course the goat trill.'

I nod once more. I raise my glass to my lips and drink, my eyes never leaving his. Go on, I think. Do go on with your triumphant phrases, your technical banter. Because I can feel myself slipping into his private world.

'The goat trill, to be sure. It's an old ornament and, mark my words, there's hardly anyone left who can still deal with it. It's produced by expelling the breath very gently and rhythmically, and perhaps you can imagine the effect this creates, at least if you do it properly: the voice opens and shuts with incredible speed and the tone, which is sustained at the same pitch, lets itself go, waives all reserve and begins to shimmer.'

I would not dare to claim that I can still follow his exact words, at this late hour. Yet I am aware that they belong to what made me weep earlier this evening. They say that music, being a language that expresses the invisible, is understood by all. Did the apostles sing at Whitsun, long ago? Singing is breath, wind, Holy Ghost. Indeed I was by no means the only one this evening to sob in my box, to sigh and surrender to a drunkenness that renders the heart generous and the sex tender.

I stare pensively at his mouth.

'But that elephant ... I mean ... how in God's name did that creature get on to the stage?'

We had arrived at the theatre at about half past nine, the performance was already under way. There was a din coming from I knew not where, offensive to my ears, while Berto led me up the two flights of stairs to his tier; he shook hands, waved genially and introduced me to red frocks, black capes, blue-shaded eyelids, square wigs and a knot of youths with amazingly long arms and legs. Glancing sideways through the open doors to the boxes, I caught sight of women and men sitting together, drinking and playing cards on the brink, as it were, of a crater of fire and light.

In the distance I could hear music.

When we entered our box, a young woman with copper-coloured hair disengaged herself from the arms of a man – a prelate, I assumed, for he wore purple. It was Angelica Margherita.

She embraced me. 'Little sister,' she said. Her throat was warm. 'Little sister. Do sit down at once. The *primo uomo* will be coming on any moment now, and just guess what he's called!'

I paused.

'Gasparino! You needn't look so surprised. He was born in the same village as you.'

'Gasparo!'

'We call him Gasparino here . . .'

In a glow of candles and mirrors I sank to my seat.

I think I will not easily forget this evening, the evening when I was separated from him by a nameless throng shouting, 'Hey, look at that!' and then, 'Shut up!' before falling silent in earnest concentration.

I looked. The setting was a palace garden, convincing enough but the shades and dimensions were so out of the ordinary that I could not but imagine myself in the Indies, the Indies or Egypt.

I listened. The orchestra in the pit, consisting of two rows of strings, two harpsichords and a small wind section, was accompanying an aria by the second or third sopranist, a male singer who was giving quite a tolerable performance in the role of despairing princess. But all eyes and ears, and the sudden gesture of one of the harpsichord players, were focused not on him because – God Almighty! – the first singer was making his entrance, there, at the vanishing point between palm trees and rocks, emerged the *primo uomo*, on horseback, no less. For an instant horse and singer were of mythic proportions. Then the animal cantered forward, sweeping past extras and ballet dancers and coming so close to the second or third sopranist that the boy, pouring forth his final series of trills, barely had time to leap out of the way. There was a burst of applause. Gasparo, still in the saddle, bowed and raised his arm commanding silence. He dismounted and then, calm and smiling, took a step forward, he wore the apparel of a king.

'He's so beautiful', I heard Angelica Margherita sigh next to me. 'So very beautiful.'

Well, it was true. At first I too, with the eye of a connoisseur, observed the soprano in his costume of woven silver. His black-rimmed eyes darted to and fro as he strode along the edge of the stage. He brushed aside his fellow singers. He greeted his friends in the stage-boxes and pulled a mocking face towards the wings where, as everyone knew, la Stradina was waiting for the love duet that was to follow. Then my attention shifted. The foreplay was over. Now for the voice.

The Creation is too vast for humans, they say, too vast and too obscure, and that man invented language for that very reason. Language, words, and all the way at the end of those words, music. God's Creation dissolved into a man-made brew. Gasparo started his aria on a high note. Soft, long-sustained and ever-swelling, it was a high F-sharp at the very least. I listened without thinking of anything in particular. Gasparo was singing a text that everyone knew. Alessandro departs with his army to the Indies. He vanquishes the most noble Poro. Poro's desperate lover tries to soften Alessandro's heart. She has the most wonderful conversations with him. In the end Poro regains his land, his lover and his liberty.

Can we weep over this intrigue?

That is up to the singer. We want the sound of passion to be high, high and of extreme virtuosity. We want artfully elaborated ecstasy. Then we can weep, not on account of the story, but on account of ourselves. Then we will be filled with joy. May virtue and love assail us from on high!

He was coming to the end of his aria. The orchestra fell silent. The singer embarked on his final cadence. Without apparent effort, without the slightest flutter in the lungs, with that Indian garden behind him and that red sky overhead, he emitted a flow of tempestuous triads and then launched into a string of hammered-out triplets so prodigious that the audience, bursting with pent-up love, went wild . . . Shouts rang out even before his feat had been accomplished.

'Gasparino! We love you! We love your throat and your mouth!'

Flowers and hand-written sonnets flew through the air and landed on the stage.

Where was I? I looked sideways out of the corner of my eye. I saw Berto wrapped up in his own bliss, Angelica Margherita half swooning in her seat, and the thin-lipped prelate mumbling 'What the devil!'

A fresh coloratura. And a portamento more ethereal than air. Then, in a fraction of a second, the singer had taken sufficient breath to sing a final, inescapable line, a spear of joy and pain that you felt in your gut.

It was over. Gone the enchantment. Loud cheering. Quizzically, the musicians tucked their violins under their chins once more.

I have lost my head yet my eyes were wide open.

*

The night wore on and everything continued as before. The unspeakably spoilt audience versed itself in the art of dreaming. At first it puzzled me to feel like an outsider. Wasn't everyone here immersed in the same reality? The reality of gods in satin breeches and long curly wigs? Of devils coming down from the sky in a cart? There was a hero in a small blood-red mantle raining blows on a dragon, all the while improvising elaborately up and down the chromatic scale ... And there were the boyish women and effeminate men and the question of sex that confuses us all.

The audience's attention was fickle, after all, they had come here also to drink and to gamble and now and then to doze. No one at all listened to the bass and the tenor. Of the three female voices only la Stradina's was considered passable. Upon hearing that Gasparino had come on again, we abandoned the roast pigeons filled with thick red conserve and hurried out of the dining-room. Leaning on the parapet in front of me I scanned the stage and yes, there he stood, the castrato in the radiant circle of his beauty, peeling an orange and looking bored. Only when la Stradina had come to the end of her song did he step forward.

... The voice, and then there was that body. The loveliest and lightest of God's gifts allied to the strong body of a man over six foot tall. I find such paradoxes appealing and in that respect I was no different from the six or seven friends and brand-new acquaintances who were transfixed with joy in their seats behind me. We are fond of equivocation, enigma, and we are especially fond of rapture. Your body is what you are and all knowledge begins with desire. For what if not for rapture?

Then suddenly I raised my hand to my forehead, the

keenest of all my recollections had flashed across my mind, and *that* was what was causing my isolation from everyone else in the opera house: the boy singer standing in a circle of light against the background of a wall in a church. I had heard this singer before. Of all those present I was the only one to have experienced that instant, to have preserved it, prevented it from trickling away, and thus able to reinsert it into the world with the utmost ease. What was the difference between then and now? Everything around me said: it is infinitesimal. No more than a breath, a sound, the leap of an octave whose doubled vibrations are barely perceptible . . .

I groped behind me, somewhat light in the head, to feel my chair. For, heaven help me, that single interval encapsulated all I knew about love, and yes, also his journey in a carriage to a medical clinic in Norcia. Your body is what you are, I thought, and I kept thinking that thought for the rest of the night, with unremitting passion, even when war broke out on stage and hundreds of cavalry, proper militiamen and not just mercenary scum, drove the horses from the royal stables on to the stage, aligned themselves in battle formation and, in a growing cacophony of trumpets and drums, started hacking at each other.

How can I let you know that I am here, hidden away, divided from you by a blinding foreground?

'I am dying,' I said to Angelica Margherita when it was all over.

We joined the crowd descending the staircase. She took my hand, squeezed my fingers gently and gave me a sidelong look.

'I must speak to him at once.'

She laughed, knowingly. 'This very night?'

'Tonight at the latest.'

'Come,' she said. 'You can breathe again. I know where to find him.'

Stepping outside we were met by a gusty November wind. We drew our capes around us, Berto's driver and servants were waiting, but Angelica Margherita looked eagerly into the darkness.

'It's only a little way. The two of us will walk,' she decided, and only agreed to be escorted by one of the servants after he had promised not to light his lantern.

'It's only a few minutes, really,' she said, sounding very pleased with herself as she steered me round a corner. 'I happen to know who's invited him and I also know he will be there.'

I think we lost our bearings from the start. We turned left, then right, and went on doing so. My sister's steps were light and quick and I found it easy to adjust my pace to hers, which was surprising because the alleys were unpaved and very dark. There was no light apart from the small red lanterns at the feet of the statues of smiling Madonnas with upturned eyes on every street corner. Each time we passed one I would pause to give a greeting, and I did not feel in the least unsafe as we walked through the maze of shadows. The natural state of the night is darkness, as everyone in the street seemed to agree, for we came across no one – whether alone or in a group, whether shuffling warily or striding past – bearing a light. And the one time a perfidious glow did loom towards us from the shadows of a small square, Angelica Margherita drew me aside in a purely instinctive reaction and shouted to make herself heard over the wind: 'Put out your lamp!', whereupon she was immediately obeyed.

But eyes grow accustomed to darkness. Open them wide and you can soon distinguish the subtle contours and half-tones of your surroundings. It was the usual scene of loving embraces, business transactions, soliciting, gambling, robbery, blackmail and various kinds of sleep. Most of the huddled shapes we saw would wake, in daylight, to recount their dreams, but one figure, with a dagger sunk up to the hilt into his gold-embroidered mantle, would not.

I had of course long since noticed that our escort had vanished.

'All the better,' said Angelica Margherita. 'What's the point anyway? I've wandered here often enough, and have never had cause to summon a bodyguard. This is a light-hearted city, its guardians are women. *Primo*, we have the Madonna, and *secondo* . . .'

She paused. She looked around her and it seemed to me that she was straining to hear something. We were standing on the corner of a street which led to a run-down square. I could make out the contours of sheds and warehouses. I could hear sails flapping, a cow lowed in the distance, a sea breeze was blowing. But then I was flabbergasted: above the sound of the wind I caught snatches of what was unmistakably a woman singing.

'... *secondo*, we have the Siren. Whenever the wind blows in from the sea she roams the city streets to bewail her lost love to every stone, every roof.'

Of course I knew the story.

The Siren's name is Parthenope. She sits beside her sister on a rocky outcrop high above the sea and for a moment you might deem the situation idyllic, for the sky is blue and green the grass under the girlish buttocks. But then the eye is drawn to the heap of bones buzzing with flies against which the sisters recline in a pose of youthful indifference: the remains of sailors lured by the Sirens' voices. It is Parthenope who first notices the black ship on the waves down below. She nudges her sister, whereupon the twosome launch into song, pure, high-pitched, and with a crescendo of maddening intensity. When the ship draws near enough to distinguish the men Parthenope is lost. For in the midst of the oarsmen, grim-faced and staunchly rowing the vessel as fast as they can, stands the man of her life, tied to the mast. And her love is requited! Handsome, fair-haired, with lightning eyes the young man listens to the luring voice telling him that knowledge equals bliss. It takes a quarter of an hour for the ship to slide past, twenty minutes at the most, and that is the full extent of Parthenope's love-life. Scarlet flushes rise on her throat. Her voice breaks. When even the dot on the horizon has dissolved into the void, she hurls herself into the sea.

And her singing voice? And her erotic desires? Can such things simply vanish without a trace?

On the coast, where her body washed ashore, there rose in the course of time a city which was named after her, but which, for reasons of fashion, was later renamed Naples.

'In a few hours there will be a market here.' It was my sister's voice beside me, and at that very moment something changed in the atmosphere. My curiosity was aroused, and I turned round. For through the narrow streets a rush of noise came towards us, which left no room at all for lyrical whispering: this was the bleating of goats.

'Come now, let's walk on,' I said, taken aback.

Divided in two, a stampeding herd charged past us on either side, still at headlong speed after being driven down from the hills by sturdy farm girls on mules anxious for a last opportunity to milk the animals before they were sold. There were also some pigs in the mêlée. And horses. And an ox with gigantic horns which slipped and fell at our feet, and scrambled upright again with a muffled bellow. I was forgetting where I had come from and where I was going.

Beaten earth pattered by satin slippers. A sleeping swine drew in its feet as we passed. A smell of excrement and fetid mud wafted towards us from the hovels as we crossed the length of the square and came upon a church. The doors were open and we could see, in the glowing depths, several shadows moving about. I caught a glimpse of gleaming eyes, an arm, a red sleeve, a bottle, a knife, and then we were swallowed up by the total gloom of an alley.

'They're escaped convicts. There are about ten or twelve of them living in the church, and they have done quite well for themselves. Because not only are they supplied with food but also, at night, carriages come to deliver their occasional boys, their girlfriends.'

'What are their crimes?'

'Everything under the sun. Robbery, embezzlement, but especially murder. An acquaintance of mine is here because he refused to take Holy Communion at Easter. The priest had him arrested at his home, but he escaped. He belongs to the Genovesi family, a likeable youth. I visit him now and then to discuss geometry.'

She paused to find her bearings. I was almost surprised to find she remembered the object of our journey. 'The Palazzo Penna, that's where Gasparino has gone. We are almost there. First we turn left, then right.'

Suddenly I became impatient, and I was evidently not the only one. Ahead of me I could hear the thump of galloping hooves and the crunch of carriage wheels rolling over the sand at full tilt. The streets widened, the gables became taller and more elaborate. At one point we had to jump out of the way and were treated to the sight of two link-boys in bright blue livery racing to a crossroads from opposite directions, their torches blazing the way for the four-in-hand stagecoaches at their heels. Neither of the gleaming vehicles ceded an inch, it seemed to me, yet each rounded the corner and disappeared from view in one fell curve. Vehicles and speed. I was soon to notice that Neapolitans are not pedestrians. They travel on horseback and in carriages – they even have themselves carried bodily – and do their utmost never to slacken their pace. I have seen how they jostle and shove, how they cut in front of each other, overtake left and right without carrying lights, and career four abreast down the via Toledo to Capo di Monte like unassailable devils.

But we had arrived. And sure enough, such a commotion all of a sudden, and so many candles at the windows of the palaces and so many torches held aloft by the coachmen. Our own manservant, too, had turned up again, and flooded the ground before our feet with light.

We reached the gate at the very same moment as Berto's carriage.

'Here already?' he cried, stepping down from his carriage, followed by his friends. He took my elbow and led me into the courtyard, then he let go in order to relieve himself among the potted pomegranate trees. Angelica Margherita, too, sank briefly to the ground.

I went ahead to the vestibule and, peering around me, climbed the stairs to the first floor. Half in a trance yet as tense as a whippet I registered the tinkling in the kitchens, the aroma of roast lamb and, guided by the sound of mandoline and guitar, I found the salon where Gasparo stood, imposing, gently rounded shoulders, surrounded by people but in fact wrapped up in his own universe, his own air, his beauty, the extravagance of his voice.

*

He laughs maliciously.

'That elephant, believe you me, was my most talented opponent this evening.'

He fixes me with his eyes, evidently I am supposed to share his laughter.

My query was of course for want of something better to say. For the sight of Gasparo coming on stage at the end of the performance with an elephant in tow and grandly bowing to acknowledge the applause beside the creature's trunk, had not for a moment increased my stupefaction.

But now I put on a face of studied interest.

'The animal was a gift to Charles by some sultan or other.'

His voice sounds more impersonal than that of a parrot.

I can feel my ears burning. It is hard not to raise my hand to cup that lovely face. I have found what I was looking for, what I have sought for years, perhaps centuries, and now I die a thousand deaths for fear of it all slipping away from me.

He leans sideways to take a glass from a tray and then says, between sips: 'Still, it was a good performance, which is actually surprising because just before the first act I thought tonight was going to be awful. There are all sorts of tell-tale signs: your shoes pinch, you feel the urge to sneeze, your lips are too dry while the air around you is too humid. So I arranged for the order of the second and third acts to be reversed. Oh, didn't you notice? It makes no difference, anyway. The sequence was changed because in Act Three I start with a patetica in G major, a rather pleasing thing with a whole series of runs and trills, nothing special really but they have to be sung on the vowel E. That was the whole point. Because the E allows one to contract the muscles around the epiglottis, which is the best way of rousing a voice that is not wholly disposed. Risky, you think? Not really. The muscles around the epiglottis operate just like the muscles around the mouth, and as I'm sure you are fully aware that your mouth is never strained by closing, only by opening wide.'

He pauses briefly, as if his own words cause him to reflect. And in that silence, that trusted bar of rest during which, as in a piece of music, nothing is lost but on the contrary all is retained, a flood of heat-rending tenderness wells up in me. I look into his earnest face. It strikes me that the skin under his eyes resembles curdled milk. The eyelashes are still tinged with blue.

His singing voice unhinged my mind, earlier this evening.

His words reassure me, for they reveal him to be human.

I lower my shoulders and listen, for the first time, to the sounds around me. Talking, laughing, someone coughs, the wind snatches at the windows, and a barcarolle starts up in the adjoining room. Doesn't madness often lurk in the most mundane places?

I say: 'Do you realize we were born in the same village?'

He looks at me in amazement.

'You and I both come from Croce del Carmine.'

My confidence grows. Here, in this exuberant salon, I am surely not the only one to make eyes at the singer, behind my lids flit the most unambiguous images. But I am certainly the only one to start reminding him calmly of the houses and paths of his village, of the Mass in the Santa Monica and the extraordinarily pleasing solo motet performed by a boy soprano during the celebration of the Eucharist.

'You stood there like a tamed angel and the rest of us in the church were struck dumb. I think you were singing a *Regina coelorum*, but whatever it was, you brought forth such turns as the village has never heard since.'

He smiles at me. I am aware of his alerted interest. The way he smiles at me – I don't know – makes me hear my own heartbeat. How will I ever regain my peace of mind? How can I have slept within close range of a volcano? I open my eyes wide and again I observe his god-forsaken beauty, his mouth and cheeks which are already mine, which I have appropriated by triggering his memory, by invoking his early childhood, the village with the peach trees, I have inflicted this on him quite unscrupulously, and now he holds me captive with a markedly searching gaze . . .

'You're quite right, it was a *Salve regina coelorum*, I recall very clearly. It was the sort of old-fashioned composition, probably by one of those Dutchmen, in which some quotation or other serves as counterpoint, and in the circumstances you couldn't possibly call it original: by way of counter melody the organ played *l'homme, l'homme, l'homme armé*, what could be duller than that. And yet it was a fantastic piece, although you couldn't tell from the notation any more, because on paper there were just chords which, if you didn't know any better, succeeded one another in stiff and wooden progression. But of course by then it had already been drummed into me that it was up to the singer to introduce the dynamics. I had been told that under the surface of a composer's bare melody lies the entire colourful range of his thoughts, and that a singer who deals properly with his voice can make this heard. Now I did not care in the least about the world of the composer, even then, colourful or not, because as far as I'm concerned the only thing that matters is what the score looks like – and that's just black and white – and other than that anything you may have in your throat. But what were you saying? You're from Croce del Carmine? Then I must be able to guess the name of your family.'

He looks down at the floor, furrowing his brow. 'No,' he then says, 'they never heard me sing there again, which may seem rather odd, because a singer is a traveller and the village is not that far away. But that's the way of things, you travel half the globe and then when you get back to Naples even a mile seems too far to go. Oh yes, Rome, Venice, Vienna, Paris, London – pleasant cities, but of course my interest lies primarily in the theatres. And the theatres range from splendid to pleasing, or at least tolerable, but now we have the San Carlo here they don't cut such a good figure any more. So you can imagine why I'm not too keen about having to leave Naples tomorrow. Oh. Hadn't you heard? Tomorrow I'm off to Genoa, to sing *Mitridate*, which could be worse, for there's a fairly good ... What is it? Why do you look so downhearted all of a sudden?'

I I

Upon waking my first thought is of a ship sailing out of port. I imagine it to be a vessel with about eight sails, the topsails struck because there is still a strong wind blowing. The voyage will not take long. Gasparo will reach Genoa in four days. I toss and turn in bed, restlessly searching for a bearable position. Yesterday was the first time in my life that I found myself talking to someone I actually wanted to get to know, not just a little, but utterly. Since yesterday I have felt an overpowering desire to immerse myself in a mystical concatenation of virtuosity, idle chatter and a very special male body whose beauty has something inhuman about it. What a quandary! Music and sex, forces have gathered within me that I cannot possibly suppress. I open my eyes, someone has entered my room. It is Faustina. I can hear her padding across the straw mat which is laid on the cold marble floor in winter. Don't bother, I say when her face and arm appear, just leave the bed curtains drawn. She looks at me knowingly and smiles. No doubt she has guessed already. Wanton, urgent fantasies, I wish I could have unrolled myself at his feet like the furry hide of an animal, but how about him? He sets sail for Genoa, my dressmaker's native town. Ha! cries Angelica Margherita as she comes in, our harbour is indeed the handsomest in the world! There is so much we could export. Silk, oil, wheat, soap, artificial flowers, but can you credit it, the only thing the world wants from us is our crowning glory, our virtuoso singers.

'By the way, the dressmaker's arrived. You must get out of bed.'

'I don't want to.'

'But you must.'

'He sailed this morning.'

'He'll be back.'

'When?'

'Before Christmas, to be sure.'

'What am I to do till then?'

She opens her arms out wide and laughs.

The bed curtains have been pushed aside. I look at the daylight, white, cool, it speaks of wind and sea air. My sister is perched on the sofa by the window, her glance flits from me to the side-table on which Faustina has left a silver tray. Angelica Margherita is sure to have breakfasted already, at her aunt's house on the quay, but still she seems to find the fresh coffee and rolls tempting. She gets up, opens the connecting door and runs down the small gallery, past the statues of Hermes and Aphrodite placed between the windows, to the dressing-room. The Genoese dressmaker is waiting by the fireplace. He accepts her warm invitation.

The three of us breakfast on bread and duck pâté; I remain in bed. The Genoese dressmaker converses with us civilly about the republic of Genoa and the kingdom of Naples. Naples, we tell him, may well be a town of plague, fire and sulphur, but the military battlefields are to be found elsewhere. We mention Lombardy, the Savoy kingdom, the foothills of the Alps, we touch on Catalonia and Flanders.

'How does war start?' we ask.

The man from Genoa eyes us in silence. He knows perfectly well that war is a question of language. It is mere dogma that drives human beings to mass together in hordes. It is mere abstraction that raises a husband and father to the level of authority. The sharper the intellect, the more efficacious the war. Neapolitans are violent, we concede, they rob and murder like the best of us. But it's a fact that people here, in this city, have for a long time taken pleasure in acquiring knowledge not with their heads but with their senses. We are followers of Apollo, but above all of Dionysus. Of course we are familiar with Aristotle, but still we are loyal to Sappho. We enjoy philosophy, appreciate science, but it is the logic of poetry that we find convincing. In this anti-papist city where Jesuits are criticized to their faces, the Inquisition did not strike root. Not one heretic was burned at the stake. Let us note in conclusion, before the Duchess of Rocca d'Evandro deigns to rise at last, that Descartes is popular in the salons of Naples, especially when there are any Frenchmen around. I think therefore I am. We nod knowingly, and don't dissolve into giggles until later.

Then I stand, stark naked, in front of the mirror. The carved frame is crowned by a leering cross-eyed satyr. My reflection, pale and wanton. It's hot in the dressing-room, a fire blazes in the grate. The dressmaker has ordered his maid to hang out the gowns. Now he watches as he waits for us to get ready. First I must put on a wine-red whaleboned bodice, Angelica Margherita must take off her dress. Faustina trots to and fro between us, babbling to all and sundry as is her custom nowadays. 'Stop staring!' she reprimands a button.

A cloud descends over my body, I can smell the scorch of freshly ironed fabric, I reopen my eyes to find my body on display in a hoop of red silk. Beautiful, so very beautiful, I hear Angelica Margherita sigh, and the sudden recollection of last night is so sharp as to be painful. Gasparo. The horse. The elephant. A sailing ship. I can feel Faustina's fingers on the skin of my back.

'Do me a favour,' she crows, tugging at the gold braid, 'and give a little.'

There is no more pleasant sensation than when the last hook is laced tight. The waist fits snugly, I can still breathe but the silk strains against my rib-cage. The dressmaker asks me to turn around. I do as he says and meanwhile ask my highly experienced sister if she has ever amused herself with anyone other than the conventional sort of gentleman or lady, with a castrato, by any chance?

She has.

'Well, how was it?'

She raised her arms. A garment of bright-yellow moiré is lowered. When her face reappears it is wearing a dreamy expression.

'His name was Raphael. It only lasted three weeks.'

I continue to stare at her. Her eyes, too, widen.

'At the slightest brush of my fingers his skin would quiver.'

'Signora?'

The dressmaker rearranges the skirt, then ties a bow around her bare throat. It is the fashion of Versailles.

*

What am I to do until then? How shall I bear it? Well, a few days later I am introduced to a Frenchman who is a guest at one of the grand houses on the Chiaia. He is undeniably special. On the way to his bedchamber you pass through an anteroom in which two tables, placed before the windows, are laden with telescopes, timepieces on silver mounts, brass measuring instruments, leatherbound books. What is that metal sphere-and-ring? It is delightful to take the two burnished objects in your hands and, surrendering to equivocation and awe, forget the world around you. When you look up your eyes meet those of the *marquis*, a young buck sent to Italy for his education, clever, gay, powdered curls cascading over the shoulders of a jacket that suits him to perfection. He laughs with amusement but not condescension, he takes your interest seriously. On a subsequent occasion he says he has found a gift for you.

'Allow me.'

'Ah . . .! *Monsieur!*'

'Upon my honour, you do me great pleasure . . .'

'The pleasure is all mine!'

The handsome book weighs heavily on your two hands. Who wrote it? Algarotti. What is the subject? The subject is Newton, but the book is entertaining none the less. You learn that the young author has written his Italian version of Newton's text with female readers in mind, his sentences light-footed and interspersed with diverting notions.

Allow me . . . Someone sucks at your throat, you laugh indulgently and a little mockingly. Your clothes are awry, they slip to the ground, you gaze into hazel eyes imploring above your face, you sigh, you lie back in a shameless but logical pose. Questions, promises, favours. You hear a whispered proposition in French – you don't understand the words but you catch the meaning, you kneel and prostrate yourself, black hair rippling across a pillow of red damask. Shall I run my hand, first the palm and then the fingertips, over the dark hairs on your chest, your satin belly, so that I will, inevitably, encounter your strong, assertive potency? The laughter has gone from your eyes, too. We have passed the stage of having fun. *Newtonianismo per le Dame*, bound in morocco, lies on a stool between the bed curtains. Now and then my eye is caught by the book, but the contents must wait. There are other insights to be gained in the *palazzo* on the Chiaia with a view of the sea where a ship, northward-bound, ploughs a furrow of foaming white waves.

*

The Chiaia is on the seafront. Everyone enjoys a drive along the boulevard, which is quite grand, bordered on one side by *palazzi*, on the other by the sea. Berto, concerned about my melancholy, had taken me out in a carriage drawn by four small swift horses. He pointed out the hills, the clouds, the sun glinting on the dome of a sanctuary. Enjoy! said the dark eyes. Among the small boats on the beach stood fishermen wearing dingy white breeches and bandannas, stooping over a net brimming with glistening life.

I sat across from him and did not move, I was boring. For days I had been impossible. At parties, playing cards, my thoughts were always elsewhere. The previous evening I had sat at a table which had been brought in, fully laden, at a quarter to midnight. I had nudged my sister beside me with my elbow. What do you know about Gasparo? Tell me about his loves.

'Wait a while,' she said. 'The day of fasting begins in fifteen minutes. Let's eat first, because they'll take the table away shortly.'

Enjoy, said her eyes, as did those of the others. The notables of the town, guests of the Duke of Mont'Allegre, tucked enthusiastically into the food. The servants' gloved hands removing the covers from the silver salvers only made the food more appetizing. How could they have melons on the menu now, at the onset of winter? Midnight came. Angelica Margherita laid her hand on her breast, gave an exhausted laugh and turned to me.

No need to tell you that Gasparino, with that gorgeous mug of his, is doted on in this city and that there is no one, man or woman, dresser or prince, messenger or *monsignore*, who does not catch their breath at the mere thought of his voice – I recall a thin-faced student priest with a goat's nose who stalked him like death itself. If you drive down the via San Carlo at night, you will always find someone staring up at the dark windows of his house. It's hard to tell what kind of flirtation has his preference. In Rome, when he was still singing female roles, there were two recently married baronesses, twins they were, bold as brass, pesky really, and they wept buckets when his contract ran out and he left the city. Here in Naples he sought the company of a woman who had two passions, the card table and love. They were together for one year. He really seemed to care for her. Then she became demanding, pathologically jealous, he couldn't go anywhere without a pair of brawny fellows turning up at his side, former seamen with gloomy faces, to protect him, so she said, from her irate husband. Gasparino made himself scarce. While he sang on the stages of Venice and London, she sat at the gaming table, elated and relieved, nowadays she is partial to fish-heads.

Dark, heady, sparkling Vesuvius wine. The day of fasting had begun and the rules did not extend to drink. Even before the harpsichord concert had come to an end there was shouting and laughter. From the green-baize tables candidates were called for a game of quadrille, the cards were of Spanish design.

Then it was as if I saw myself from a distance. A Hollander, young, with startlingly blue eyes, spread his cards out in a fan and looked at his partner in confusion. This partner was very beautiful, delicately built but with generous shoulders, a silk rose behind one ear set off the mass of black hair. It was the sopranist Tonio, known for cross-dressing. Everyone had been following the affair with amusement. The Hollander trailed after the object of his affections through the salons with the candid ardour of his northern mien, he had no idea.

Tonio laid down a card, he won. He played a second, and was lucky again. The Dutchman lost and nodded meaningfully to his beloved. Although his command of the language was far from perfect, he knew what the custom was when you first lost at cards to a lady: her winnings – a mere nine carolines in this case – are to be delivered to her house the following day, wrapped in a ribbon costing at least one gold ducat.

Hello, how's it going? It was Berto's voice rising above the hubbub of the crowd from which one person was absent.

I was extremely ill-humoured.

He pressed my fingers and felt how cold and clammy they were. A moment later I was warming my hands over the glowing embers of a brazier. I nodded. Berto had proposed a refreshing drive along the Chiaia the following day.

The afternoon light streamed in through the carriage windows. Everything reeled and swayed, the driver drove the horses at a fast pace. My eyes scanned the ships riding at anchor in the bay. They seemed very distant. Berto was in an irrepressibly good mood. Do you see those geese? he asked. I knew that he was embroiled in a brand-new affair. His eyes swept from the mountain slopes to the sky high above the sea. Why should I begrudge him his infatuation, his youthful Sicilian lover with the narrow, arrogant face? To anyone under the influence, the world is close at hand. You

touch and are touched in turn. You can put your hands
around a bird in the sky. We reached the end of the
boulevard. The carriage slowed down and turned in a
wide semicircle. Now, looking ahead I could now see the
smoking Vesuvius far away in the distance.

'Soon we will arrive at the house where a friend of
mine is staying,' said Berto. He reached for his hat. 'A
Frenchman. You will like him.'

We turned into a courtyard. In the anteroom filled
with telescopes and measuring instruments a foreigner
bent over my hand.

He has curly eyelashes, I thought, to console myself.

*

The days shorten, I am suspended in time. The evening
is scarcely different from the morning, day almost
indistinguishable from night. Why not resign myself to
longing for one who is absent but bound to return? I
exist in a vacuum, which I fill with seeing, hearing,
smelling, tasting, feeling. There is no lack of temp-
tations. I sleep when the fancy takes me, I go out when
the fancy takes me. When Berto and I entertain guests,
I flirt with the entire table, and after dinner we make
music. My French friend is among the regular guests.
Sometimes he spends the night at our house. On other
occasions – when the fancy takes me – I order the
carriage to be hitched.

He always receives me in high spirits. While he slips

one hand under the hair on my neck, he turns the pages of a book with the other. We sit in the anteroom, a wood fire warming our backs, and talk about the force that holds the moon in orbit: take note, it is by the same force that a stone falls to the ground! I am impressed by his progress in Italian. He says the credit for this is due to the maestro who comes twice a week.

'Immaculate buttocks,' he whispers later, without a trace of a foreign accent. 'Oval in shape, resilient, firm, smooth. May I ask you to raise your foot a little?' I have noticed that he, like so many men, likes observing the boy in his women.

Take that time we rode to Pozzuoli.

He had said: 'Tomorrow morning I will ride to Pozzol to admire the local antiquities.'

'Pozzuoli,' I said, and offered to accompany him. It took him a while to comprehend that I required neither a side-saddle nor a page.

'All right. Wonderful.' He thought it would be fun. 'I'll take a roast turkey along for a picnic.'

Mounted on a Neapolitan thoroughbred, I appeared at his gate – his eyes narrowed – I was wearing riding breeches and a suitable jacket. 'Ha, there you are,' he said finally. Riding through a pitch-dark tunnel, we left the city at a gallop.

Panoramic views, clear weather. We went up a rocky path and saw ruins, deer, birds and tombs: when we came to the ancient Roman road I happened to be riding ahead again, and my companion was a little taciturn. In the Grotto of the Sybil he embraced me.

'I must have you now, this very minute.'

'Right now?' I laughed and looked around me. We had found the spot with some difficulty. A stone vault, high, spacious, hidden, a strange breeze. This was where Apollo's priestess . . .

'Drat!'

My Frenchman had discovered an Englishman. I stepped aside. A lord with ginger eyebrows, who like us had followed the directions on the map, stood in the entrance to the cave. He approached and introduced himself. What was more natural than for us to proceed on our tour as a threesome?

Temples and churning lakes, gathering clouds in the late afternoon, supper at the inn, the journey home in the gloom and downpour and the warm exchange of farewells with the English lord, those were our preoccupations until the moment the door of the *palazzo* on the Chiaia finally closed behind us. Then my friend, worn out, soaked to the skin, looked into my eyes. Without speaking he reminded me of what he had wanted earlier and what I had been ready to give him. There was to be no visit to the opera that evening.

*

For that is what I want, the hour, the place, the action, I want to go to the San Carlo all the time. My days may be as hectic as they will, I know of one event that contrives to hold its own night after night, almost without interruption.

'Not again? You can't be serious! What for?' my friend bursts out, and by the time we arrive at the blue-and-gold opera house one of the celebrated soprano arias has just begun.

'It's the same performance until the middle of December,' he rambles on. 'The same old story, day in, day out.' We sink into the plush upholstery.

'What do you mean, sir, by the same day in, day out?' I say. 'No one ever sings the same aria twice.'

He beckons a Turkish valet sporting a bushy moustache. 'Oysters and a bottle of Lacrima Christi.'

The voice rises. I can dream the melody. Throughout the first part the singer follows the notes with precision.

'And later on, after the next part, you can be sure the whole thing will start all over again.' My friend stretches his legs good-naturedly.

'You are the deafest man in the world!' I say and permit him to withdraw to the gaming-room.

From my dark corner I listen to the soprano, a twelve-stone fellow with an eagle on his head launching into the aria's da capo, the ornamented repetition, the second time round being to the first like a story to the facts. I come alive. This is what I love. Intonation, pathos, persuasion. At the start of the cadence the entire orchestra relaxes. Centuries go by. This is not repetition, this is a blissful protraction of time.

'So what do you think of the Frenchman?' I ask my sister the following day. 'He says it's odd for the role of Achilles to be sung by a soprano.'

'How do you mean?'

She stands still on the steps of the Maria del Carmine and fumbles in her coat pocket for some coins. On this sunny winter's day we make our way to the church to visit the oldest olive-wood Madonna in the city. Faustina says there has been a fiery blush on her cheeks since last Sunday. We are not the only ones to have heard about the miracle. In a crowd of pilgrims, epileptics and dogs with glowing eyes we reach the portal. At our feet a woman is struggling up the steps on her knees, leaning on an elbow each time she lowers her head to lick the stone slabs.

'How do you mean?' asks Angelica Margherita. 'Surely he must know that a bass or tenor can't reach those high notes, can't achieve the power, the speed?'

A masked beggar accepts our alms. We push against a door and are engulfed by the darkness of a vault. Under a fiery arched window stands the Virgin, brown, old and patient. Her cheeks are rosy and the matt whites of her eyes turn slowly to and fro.

'He's surprised about the love duets,' I tell Berto later that afternoon. 'He considers it strange for the two singers to be identical in type of voice.'

My husband mumbles absent-mindedly. Identical, what? He has just woken from his siesta and is sitting on the edge of the bed. Tonight he will wear a new outfit, brilliant as the polestar, and will engage me in conversation about Ptolemy. Now his shirt is crumpled. Waiting for the coffee to heat up, he stares vacantly in the direction of a small display cabinet on the wall. His favourite collection, statuettes and red-figure vases. The locals have always known about a city in these parts, an antique city buried along with its entire history under the ashes of the volcano. May I show you my prize find? Berto asked me one day. He laid a shepherd's pipe carved from bone and ivory in my hands. Shall I tell you who, in my view, is the god of music? Who are you thinking of, dearest? Of serene Apollo and his lyre? I am more in favour of Hermes, who is both god and man and deft with his fingers. It isn't the thought that counts in the world, after all, but action. Everyone knows Apollo's lyre was fashioned by Hermes, the lyre and indeed also the flute.

That Friday night the *marquis* sparkles at me.

'Now this was really good!'

His French soul is amused. He writhes in his seat, rubs his hands, hunts for his tobacco and sees that his companions in the box share his mood: all mouths are eagerly upturned, all hands are clapped.

'Good good good!' he repeats.

He raises his opera glasses and adjusts the lenses in

order to bring up close the face of the maestro behind the harpsichord on the right: the composer, he presumes.

Tonight's serious opera has been interrupted by a comic intermezzo. A brazen maidservant lords it over the master of the house and flatters and manipulates the fool in clearly articulated Italian. Woman is woman, man is man, and the music is poignant and adequate. A new style emerges, a rainbow in the sky.

'I must speak to him! I must have a copy of the score.'

I follow his enthusiasm indulgently. They should hear this in the Académie Royale, he tells me. Clarity and simplicity, and away with the convoluted trappings of the fugue, of the counterpoint, which, if you ask me, is in even worse taste than a Gothic church portal!

Shaking my head, I lay my fingers on his wrist. No, that grey-haired fellow with the yellow jutting jaw is not the composer. Pergolesi is said to have been a beautiful young man, full-lipped. And don't think this genius who died so lamentably young, this precursor, this darling who was poisoned by his rivals from Rome, was averse to the virtuoso aria.

'In about ten days' time one of his serious operas will open here,' I say.

In ten days' time! I open my eyes wide and lean back into my chair because the curtain is rising, my friend saunters into the foyer, leaving me to savour the third act starting up for the umpteenth time. Half in dreams,

I observe the scene, the all too familiar ruins, the all too familiar lush vegetation of bluish-green, and I think: later, in ten days' time; something new will come of all this. And while the music streams towards me from all angles, now soft then loud, sometimes in descending then in ascending rhythms, in musical beats which rather than measuring time render it perceptible in the beating of your own heart, I think: in a moment, in this very place, strutting like a rooster, the love of my life will appear. The new opera programme has been published in the *Gazzetta di Napoli.* I can sense the passage of time in the fitful coursing of my blood. You should take care, Faustina admonishes me, you're getting more scatterbrained by the day. Posters have gone up all over town with the name of the lead soprano printed in giant capitals. The winter sky darkens. Silver birds skim over the waves. One day someone tells me that Gasparino is back in Naples.

III

'. . . after bar twenty-four you get an awkward passage with very rapid quintuplets rising higher and higher, from F sharp, to G sharp, to A, and then it gets tricky, you see. If you don't keep track of the notes at that dizzying speed and at that height, the whole thing will collapse, then it won't be music you're hearing but, well, it'll be more like a coughing fit. Know what I mean? Right. That recurring leap from the middle F sharp to the high B is the most important statement. Whatever you slip in by way of trills, glissandi and repeating thirty-seconds, the word itself still has to be pronounced on F sharp and B. What does it matter, you may think, just that one word? Because you think you're listening to the pleasing vibration of vocal cords and you forget that that may well be so, but that, as far as vibration is concerned, the violin or the harpsichord can serve perfectly well, and they're charming instruments, but they do not speak words. They pretend to, and their imitation goes quite a long way, but as for vowels and consonants, no, because those you form with the mouth. That frenzied soaring, those grace notes and the swelling and falling away – nothing but words, too, there's no denying, words broken free from their moorings, if you like, on a spree for all I care, but for words you need tongue and lips . . .'

He pauses for a moment.

Then he adds: 'And teeth of course.'

'No,' I say, 'no teeth for now, please.' And I bend over and bring my face close to his until our lips touch. I kiss him delicately, expertly. Oh such enticement, the warm singer's mouth once more, practised, an orifice now closed. I push gently against the upper lip and explore the corners, those shadowy folds where the secret of closed mouth or parted lips lies hidden. In the midst of my foray I look up. He is impassive. His eyes still glow, but the eagerness, it seems to me, has dimmed.

'Taste this,' I venture. 'M, the consonant formed by the lips alone.'

His bed is no longer strange territory. We have abandoned all reserve. My naked back is familiar with the satin blanket. I need not open my eyes to know that I am in a pleasantly heated room with fitted closets and framed paintings. Dark window-panes glitter, it is December. Our meal has left us light-headed, drifting in the warmth of the late afternoon, we are drawn to the bed. Forgive me, I say, but muscatel wine for dessert makes me languid and giddy. I have touched his face, his lips, I have unbuttoned his shirt.

'Part them . . .'

My tongue slips inside. I shut my eyes, this is where I belong. I encounter a self-contained universe lined in soft warm membranes, the tongue an emotionless animal, a wholly autonomous being, lying in complete relaxation on the floor. Not uncompliant, just a little reticent perhaps. But isn't this the same tongue that, night after night, offers generous, exhilarating gifts for all to hear?

I touch his upper teeth, on the inside, where the hard palate begins.

'D, T,' I mutter. 'Consonants formed by light, con-genial pressure behind the upper teeth.'

Each mouth has its own taste, which you can't generally tell by looking. I once knew a sea captain with a blond moustache and ruby lips whose mouth tasted of wool.

Gasparo's mouth tastes of young, sparkling wine.

I ponder. I try another tack.

'N,' I say. 'L . . . R . . . Especially the R requires the tongue to behave in an original way, rather like a delicately calibrated mechanism for switching from slack to rigid . . .'

He likes what I'm saying. He laughs out loud, his face is suddenly full of animated movement, and so is his body. He pushes me away, rolls over on to his elbow, grasps my wrist beside my loosened hair and observes me with renewed interest.

I am covered by his white chest.

'A' – he comes into action – 'is open and round in shape.'

This kiss is ravishment. My wordless cry of rapture (Ah!) is also one of astonishment. Such command? Such virility? Not even when, an hour ago, or two hours, who takes heed of time, his desire manifested itself visibly . . .

He whispers, his lips above mine: 'It's not only your mouth you must open wide, but also, and in particular, your throat. To articulate this important vowel properly you must, I tell you, completely relax your tongue.'

I obey. I am learning. My head is pressed into the pillow.

He persists: 'More passive, more relaxed. Listen, you must banish all thought of other sensations.'

Respiration. Silence and stifled throaty sounds. Oh! (Lips rounded, interior space intact.) That the most intimate recesses of my mouth are being explored, touched and brought to life – points, arches, agreed: you imagine this to be the dome of a great vault – puts me in a mood of diligence and concentration that I can feel in my innermost being.

But personally I would prefer, now that we are caught up in didactics, to stray a little.

Our breathing is no longer synchronized. Our oral configuration has been disturbed. The Italian vowel E, he tells me, is an evolution of the vowel A, the mouth modifies its shape slightly, becoming smaller in size, and how do you achieve that? Virtually nothing. You draw the upper and lower jaws slightly together, and that's it. Tears spring to my eyes. My attention does not wander, but appears to contract . . . the vowel I is the smallest of all, small, yes, but what a tingling sensation at the base of the nose . . . behind the pursed lips sits the U, like an eye bulging from its socket . . .

I lose track. Such exertions! Vowels, hollow syllables, moulds for words: what is entering my bloodstream is no ordinary language, but language raised to the nth degree. Drowning in words, I flounder about, stammering: 'Gasparo, dear God, if we . . . I mean . . .'

My eyes have taken on a dumb, ecstatic expression.

He has let go. He is lying on his back, arms folded under his head, legs flung wide.

Awed by the massive tranquillity of that luxuriant naked body at my side I breathe out, haltingly.

'What's really essential . . .'

That voice again, bland, monotonous, no more eloquent than a block of wood.

'. . . is that tiny point, right at the centre of your mouth, that is essential. If you can feel your voice vibrating that one hidden *puntino* you can be sure you've got it right.'

He looks sideways, assessing my reaction with an almost cunning expression. For a moment I gaze into the dark-rimmed eyes. Then, gently, I lay my hand on his small, fleshy sex.

*

I had found myself in his carriage towards midday. The church was still in complete chaos. Gasparo had lost his temper during the concert, there had been an ugly scene, too, for the organist, Signore Raimond, had had to be taken away on a stretcher after the *Miserere*, true, his performance had been abominable. When the nobles, shopkeepers and vagrants that made up most of the audience caught sight of the constables entering the church, there was an outcry. Madness! Out of their minds! How dare they attempt to arrest the singer with the most beautiful voice ever heard by man! The crowd was galvanized by the prospect of wholesale defiance and insurrection. Cheers and yells, jackets were unbuttoned, in the windswept open portal teetered the aged, fastidious Princess Belmondo, screaming like a fish-wife. Leave him alone!

Gasparo, meanwhile, was a paragon of composure. He sauntered from the main altar towards the sacristy, listened absently but graciously to the people crowding round, and caught sight of me. On an impulse, I believe, he stepped forward. He had not seen me since his trip to Genoa.

'It's getting hellish cold in here. No one seems to mind, but I've had just about enough. It'll take a minute to get my coat, my music and my manservant.'

I said nothing, I just stared. Then he told me his carriage was waiting at the bottom of the steps. 'Let's go and have a bite to eat.'

The next thing I knew the church was receding. And so was the square. And so, behind the bevelled glass of the carriage window, the house-fronts fell away, the constables had drawn back in glum silence, their weapons an embarrassment now.

'Can you tell me what's the matter with those people?' Gasparo had asked. He had held out his hand to help me into the carriage.

Fever. The rush of love. His utterly beautiful features for me alone. We turned into the via del Duomo, I gave him an encouraging look. Believe me, there is heaven on earth. Like now, for instance. The ground swayed under my feet. All my troubles took a rest. My hunger no longer consumed me, it nourished me. My yearning was not melancholy, it was bliss. Soon my thirst would invoke the next certainty. Fill my glass. Embrace me.

I glanced briefly towards the cold, shadowy city. Outside the carriage was the underworld, shrouded, endless. Inside: *terra incognita*. What manner of discoveries lay ahead? Gasparo was wearing a thick greatcoat and a cocked hat. I had asked him something about the concert. While he answered my question I thought: we are on our way to your house and, no need to beat about the bush, to your bed. The most precarious part of making love is the clothing, certain items of which must be disposed of at some point. The way you do so is not without importance. I know it is wise, in certain circumstances, to postpone the moment of discarding my tight-fitting cherry-red bodice.

He said: 'It's a perfectly good mass, very musical and there's nothing wrong with the symphonies, but they do need a bit of fire. And well, devil take it, those cellists, did you hear those idiots play?'

Not really, no. I hadn't really been present at all, there in the aisle, not for the first quarter of an hour at any rate. I could feel the crowd, I could smell the incense as it swirled into the dome, I could see the orchestra striking up, but my sense of hearing was suspended. The cellos, as I recall, were played by two ungainly musicians who shook energetically as they handled their bows, the fingers on the hair, the thumb on the wood.

'And the oboe: in and out of time.'

Eight singers had risen to their feet. The one closest to where I was sitting was Gasparo. He stood poised on the uppermost step by the altar, his boots shiny and his cheeks flushed, ready for the fray; he waved and nodded to some familiar faces in the front rows, he was back in town. Yes, but I needed time to find my bearings. I was lagging behind. His presence, there beside the organ, was not quite in step with time, I felt, and so, for the moment, I continued to see him as an unforgettable memory. Why this time-lapse? How can I bear the waiting . . . ?

They launched into the *Kyrie*. God help me, better lyrics do not exist. I sat back in my pew and my ears were opened.

These singers, eight men among whom there were several tending towards the plump, sing according to an old tradition. Composers can write what they will, it is the mode of singing that transforms the written notes into inexplicable joy. The singers strengthen or weaken a tone. They accelerate. They produce ornaments to the most curious effect. It is the task of the lead soprano to draw the whole word towards him from time to time, in a crystalline pianissimo, and to remind the public that goodness and beauty go together.

'But Don Raimond was the worst prat of all.'

The organist irritated him. The man played too loud, he made mistakes, but if Gasparo had just gone ahead with his part nothing much would have gone wrong. The *musico*, however, began casting sidelong looks, he frowned, puffed up his chest. After three bars of rest, during which he turned to face the organ squarely, emphatically marking time all the while, he resumed his solo in an uncommon, syncopated rhythm, knowing full well that this would make the organist really sweat. And so it did. For seconds on end the gilded pipes did nothing but wheeze, splutter, falter, then at last the parts came together after a fashion and the singer, in a parody of gratitude, made a small bow. Falling and rising harmonies, a modern sixth chord, odd, out of place, and yet again a slither in a high register, which was duplicated forcefully and with undeniable artistry by the soprano. The piece, by no means flawless, drew to a close. Relief in the church, amusement. Then the choir and full orchestra took over, giving the organist behind his elaborately carved instrument time to ponder revenge. And the opportunity duly arose. The next soprano solo was ruined not from lack of skill, but with subtle mastery: it is possible, by employing the reed-stop with the piercing, strident register known as *vox humana*, to blast the timbre of a soprano to smithereens. Gasparo threw down his music. He was flushed with anger. But the skirmish behind the organ was largely screened from view by the pipes set up on three sides of a square, the congregation saw little more than how it ended. *Signore* Raimond, bleeding profusely, hove into view and collapsed limply on the stone floor, his wig askew.

'His leg is fractured,' someone behind me said.

Two men with a stretcher advanced up the aisle.

A church full of people. A mass. Sensation and devotion keep each other occupied and go round in circles. Which turn would this extraordinary, incomprehensible event take next? The incense burners were swung again and the canons trailed back to their seats in the semicircle behind the altar. Introspection. The altar bell chimed like the bell round the neck of a lamb. Is it really necessary to comprehend everything all the time? I patted my breast but did not bow my head: the singers, in a forgiving mood like brothers burying the hatchet, launched into the *Agnus Dei*. One of them, on the left, finding himself to be in excellent voice, innocently set about making that clear to all. Self-portrait. Exercise in fellowship.

I am enchanted by the mischievous look in his eyes and by his fabulous technique.

I listen, not only with my ears.

I look.

The light in these carriages is always somewhat diffuse. One is boxed in by glass and velvet. After crossing the piazza Gesù at full tilt we fell silent, and I took the opportunity to scrutinize him. I am avid for understanding. Always have been. I was born with the need to understand.

Gasparo, his body turned towards me in a three-quarter pose, stared straight through me. Eyebrows, temples and eyes shaded by his hat. I observe this portrait of a man, I take in the coat, fur collar, shirt, the hand resting on the knee, as if they made up an ingenious theorem which for once required no effort to memorize. He gave me a sympathetic look: a stifled sigh had escaped me. We had arrived. This is my house. My agile manservant, who sprinted beside the carriage for some distance before leaping on to the running board at the back to get his breath back, will fold down the steps for us to alight.

We walked across thick carpets to a corner room with a connecting door, where a table had been laid for the midday meal.

*

It is the first time I see him unclothed. He is lying at my side, on the down-filled bed, the perfect proportions of his body within direct reach, and I too have taken everything off except my red bodice. My breathing is fast and shallow, I want to remain calm, I breathe more quickly than he. This irresistible male body, the most beautiful I have ever seen – if I cannot go on touching him for the rest of my life, the sun need not bother to shine – undoubtedly feels cosseted and warmed, but is still reticent. Come with me, he said a moment ago, it's more fun to lie down. Let's take the plum grappa with us. Let's take our shoes off.

Never had I seen such a body before. Until now men had always possessed hard, exposed forms, I enjoyed surrendering to their single-minded urgency, and the tickling sensation of their body hair could inspire me to do the silliest things. Gasparo is soft, white, curved. His skin is hairless. I open my arms. I am speechless, but it's not surprise. His portrait had long ago cast, physically, its spell on me.

Shut your eyes, I say, open them again. Can you feel

this? Do you want me? Do you love me? Although I am sorely tempted to take that majestic white landscape between my thighs, to mould, knead, implore, I do not lose sight of the old rule: not too much fuss the first time, be tender but not too technical. Just radiate happiness, why not admit that in the case of true love it is essentially the most mundane movements that are erotically the most stimulating? I lean on my elbow. I restrain myself. Instead of looking for signs of rising desire I take a lock of his hair – his own hair, not the wig – between my fingers. It's thick and glossy like that of a woman.

But with a woman it's different. Kissing her body (and feeling her breasts nudge against yours), means kissing a gorgeously magnified version of yourself. I have a bosom friend who can tell at a glance when I have a craving for spaghetti with cheese, say, or indeed something else. Gasparo throws back his head. It's as if he's proffering his body to me. You are charming, he says, charming, and a little strange.

His body is not that of a woman. Though his skin is velvety and his nipples slightly raised, yet there, almost concealed by the tight curls of pubic hair, languishes a milk-white member, which looks small against the scrotum that feels so sturdy and plump in my cupped hand that you'd almost forget there's something missing. I kiss, do this and that, I die of love, the boyish member becomes characteristically tumescent. When I look up, he draws my throat towards him. I can feel his heart. He gazes at me with longing, deference, and gentle mockery.

Tell me what to do.

Embrace me, I reply. Untie my bodice by working your fingers around the hooks on the back and salute my complete nakedness. Do you realize the dilemma I'm in? The concentration of sensitive spots on the skin of the back makes it very tempting to lie prone with my face in my arms and so get you all over me. But I want to look at you, I want desperately, when the time comes, to see your eyes. That's it, then, I'll turn on my back. Embrace me and grant me my wish: look at me while the sinuous rolling of my thighs brings you exactly in place, inside my warmth where, again to your surprise, it is all sensation. The proverbial missionary position has its merits, don't you agree? I know of only one embrace that is to be preferred, but we won't go into that now, my darling. Move, push, couple, as you see it is not difficult to possess me entirely, I tilt my hips a little and play my interior muscles while you go straight up and down, there, you are a manly mount indeed, our ride proceeds in a mesmerizing, monotonous rhythm culminating not in infinity but in a vertiginous moment of emptiness. You won't mind if I switch, in the meantime, from words to other typical sounds?

Out in the street the light is fading. The glow in this small room, coming from a blazing fire and flickering candles, is mirrored in the windows. We are together, alone. A sea of reflections divides us from the city. People walk by under the windows, doors are opened and shut, the siesta is ending, sounds rise.

Yet the rattle of a barrel rolling over the cobbles cannot reach us.

And a dog howls in vain.

While neighbours quarrel in sign language, the full weight of Gasparo's body presses down on my ribs.

Then suddenly a band of street musicians strikes up in front of the house. A three-part psalm sung by a troupe of castrati seeps through the wall and the window. We don't listen, of course. You can find such beggar choirs made up of rejected singers all over Naples. They crowd the market place, they advance in procession across the city squares, they flock to the taverns at supper-time to provide background music, their voices high-pitched and their chins beardless. We do not listen.

But the voices are there, persisting. The cries, long-drawn-out, stylized, besiege us with their mysterious signals, taking possession of our lungs, our bellies, whether we like it or not, drawing us into a dark but not unfamiliar world close by, a world of fear and pleasure, of passion, rage, melancholy and all sorts of things that have happened or could happen. Your body is what you are. These singers, without exception singled out when mere choirboys in a village church, wearing lace-edged surplices, still of slight build, know only one thing in life. Muscles, breathing, throat. Singing is intimate behaviour which for once is not kept secret. The *musico* volunteers to stand before a nameless audience and give a breathtaking demonstration of arrogance and restraint and endlessly polished modulations, oblivious to the world around him, truly oblivious, and so to touch extreme emotion in public.

The promise gathers momentum.

Shock and joy.

I can see him come. His pupils contract. Seeing him come makes little fiery tongues dart up all over my heart. Like the sacred heart of Jesus.

*

I asked him if he remembered our village.

'Of course I do.'

'So what do you remember?'

'The volcano,' he said, 'the vineyards, the September clouds, the fallow fields after the harvest where you could trap snakes and where the sun shone directly into your eyes at the end of the day.'

I asked him about his family and he said that he could picture his mother's mirrored wardrobe and also the way she used to lean in the doorway. How delightful it was when she strode, talking, to his bedside and sat with him for a while, her skirt spread out over the coverlet. He had got on well with his older brothers, who wore

neckerchiefs and boots. They were boisterous and cheerful and did not mind in the least that their father always
took him, Gasparo, with him when he went hunting in
the pale light of dawn. The youngest son was the father's
favourite.

'. . . which doesn't mean to say that he always gave
me what I wanted.'

He looked at me for a while in silence. Now that the
afternoon was drawing to a close I knew him so well
that I could guess his thoughts.

'Your father gambled,' I said.

'I know.'

'He used to play cards with my father.'

'Yes.'

'And he won from him. He always won, if you ask
me. Except that time when my father persuaded him to
raise the stakes with something extraordinary, something of great value. Then, that one time, he lost.'

Gasparo yawned. My patter was of no interest to him.

'I rather liked your father,' he drawled, raising his head
from my shoulder. He changed position. 'I remember very
clearly that it was he who first mentioned my career.'

Hereupon Gasparo told me the following story.

It had been after vespers. On the baking hot square
in front of the church my father, his eyes brimming
with tears, had stopped the young Gasparo Conti to
explain that if he wished, he could look forward to the
kind of life beside which real life would pale.

'You're already peering over the fence. With just a little sacrifice and effort you'll step right over it.'

My father had stayed at his side, by turns reasoning and keeping gravely silent, until they reached the spacious kitchen where his friend Benedetto Conti sat eating a lamb chop smothered in wild mushrooms. The two fathers conversed, disagreed vehemently, reconciled their differences, and became drunk.

'But my father was adamant,' said Gasparo. 'He refused to believe that I wanted to go ahead with the operation, the sooner the better. What are you doing? Do you always fidget with people's hair like that?'

'Yes,' I said. 'It is an obsessive habit.'

Then one day Conti had called his youngest son to his side. It was after the midday meal, he was resting in his easy chair on the patio, his eyes already shut.

'After my nap,' he had said, 'I want to speak to you about going to Norcia.'

'The funny thing was,' said Gasparo, 'that I wasn't in the least surprised.'

The previous evening he had seen his father leave the house around eleven. It was a warm night with a clear moon and a fan-shaped cloud hanging over the orchard. For some obscure reason everything seemed like a magic confection to the boy. His father, striding down the path without greeting, was not quite his father, the milk churns waiting under the eave of the barn were strange milk churns, in the brushed sky floated a cloud that came from the Virgin knew where.

All right, I thought, so much for the world. Reality, no less. The posturings of fate trying to conceal its true designs.

Gasparo had watched his father until he was out of sight, then he had gone inside to say his bedtime prayers.

Conti awoke from his doze. He opened his eyes.

'The day after tomorrow,' he said, 'Your mother is already packing.'

And early one morning Gasparo endured the tears of his family – his mother wore a soft, corn-coloured dress – he pushed the dog away and jumped into the carriage ahead of everyone else, and he did not attempt to construe the mild grey light above the farmhouse as a token of farewell for ever.

'Did you really not mind?' I asked.

'Not as far as I remember.'

'Didn't you cry at all?'

'No.'

He held out his glass. I filled it. Glasses, teacups, bottles, sheets, I thought, generally refer to home and family, to festive speeches at a table decked with the family silver.

The operation had not been too taxing. Gasparo had submitted willingly to the hands of dedicated strangers.

He was given a glass of liquid to drink in a whitewashed cell. Have you drunk it all? Didn't you like the taste? Strangers observed him with something like concern. It was supposed to make you drowsy. He became drowsy. The room started to wheel around him. Is this what you want, what you really want? someone asked, in keeping with the rules. Since the operation is not without lasting effects, the boy must give his consent, nothing is to be done against the child's wishes. Gasparo shut his eyes in assent, reopened them, saw the assistant's hands coming towards him, felt the thumbs press against his throat, exerting just the right amount of pressure to slow down the flow of blood to the brain but not stop it completely, and he regained consciousness surrounded by five or six other convalescent boys in a ward, where he would be nursed with onion soup and red wine until he was strong enough to undertake the voyage to Naples, to the kingdom by the sea where he, although not an orphan, would be lodged in one of the four orphanages, one of the four *conservatorios* which housed bands of very special children in the warmest part of the building, on the top floors.

I listened to him, my eyelids growing heavy. For all the monotony of his voice, the most luminous images floated behind my eyes. It was hard to tell whether I was dreaming or awake. Probably dreaming. Wasn't it the logic peculiar to dreams that caused grievous and even bloodstained images to dissolve into a tender muddle of happiness?

'Come now!' Gasparo had said a moment ago. 'Is that what you think? No no, I didn't feel sorry for myself at all.'

I sighed contentedly. A clock struck somewhere in the depths of the house. If I cannot stay with him for ever . . .

Drifting back from the brink of sleep I heard Gasparo explaining all about the essentially reasonable madness of an aria in Hasse's *Cleofide*.

'. . . Then I always take a look first to see what the possibilities are. The tempo is adagio, the movement is in eighths and the opening motif is tra – tatata-tá ta ta, nothing special about that, you might think, but it does happen to encapsulate the entire structure of a molto legato melody which proceeds, by way of the staple *vocalises*, leaps, broken chords, to a second section which is not only in a different time – a switch from common time to three eighths – but also requires a different way of singing, because here every syllable is assigned its own note. Right, then comes the da capo, and everyone knows that the whole piece, if it is willing, simply becomes one great hand-held explosion. As a singer you see how far you can go. And that's always over the top, of course, sometimes just a tiny bit, but usually as far as you can possibly go. Take a fermata: if you execute a full messa di voce by swelling and softening more slowly and more excruciatingly than is, in principle, possible, you will feel good and bad at the same time, how else can I put it, no, believe me, then it's like God and the devil being in complete agreement. Ah well, you work your way through the opening phrase as lightly and fluently as you can, grace notes and turns on the first beat, trills, too, on the weak notes. And the next sentence brings plenty of syncopation, and . . .'

IV

The rain has been pouring down all day and I still haven't seen Gasparo. That this is more than I can bear goes without saying, but there was a dress rehearsal at the San Carlo this afternoon, and his good humour of late induced my beloved to present himself there most amenably to sing a few bars. Tonight is the première of Pergolesi's *Olimpiade*, and Gasparo is starring as Megacle, the hero, the prince. My excitement mounts.

This morning Angelica Margherita and I waited for our French friend to accompany him to the royal palace. All the tourists get themselves invited there sooner or later. Our *marquis* was charmed by the Farnese paintings, he inspected the furnishings of the silk-walled salons and noticed that there was no bed in the king's apartment. That's right, we explained, Charles sleeps in his wife's bed. The two majesties are young, little more than children still, and so they need warmth. As a result, in fact, the little queen recently became pregnant, although she has never had a period.

'How weedy he looks. What a horse-face.'

Our companion looked from the antechamber towards the table where Charles and his wife were dining in public in keeping with Spanish etiquette.

'He's not much of a talker.'

He had been introduced to the well-nourished king. It was true that Charles had kept his jaws virtually clenched when a troupe of foreigners came past, bowing and scraping. We discovered the Dutch baron. While we admired his brown-piped knee-length jacket, we heard the king ask him something about the manufacturing process of Gouda cheese, we heard the young man with the close-set colourless eyelashes maintain something about pedigree cows and damp, bright green grass.

'Fantastic, but he must be out of his mind.'

Our Frenchman again, later in the afternoon when we went to Portici for a walk in the woods in spite of the drizzle. This royal hunting estate can be poached by all and sundry, there is no one to stop them. We chanced upon Charles himself, in the company of a raffish old man carrying his gun. We were permitted to join the twosome for an hour or so. Charles started taking potshots at birds, often hitting them in full flight, of the rabbits venturing out of their burrow he did not miss a single one.

'They look beheaded.'

The Virtuoso

The buildings of Naples. The roofs flat, without
cornice or tympanum. We returned to the city in the
mauve dusk and, as our calash slowed down at the Porta
Anticaglia, we were forced to a halt by two beggars
standing squarely in our path.

'*Canaille!* Vermin!' grumbled our friend as we
snapped our purses and shut the door of the vehicle.

He gave me a piqued look. I said nothing. He had
looked at me that way all day. My sister and I exchanged
glances.

'What are you thinking?' he persisted.

That your jealousy irks me. That I find it in bad taste
to confuse friendship with love. Why do you pull such a
sour face? We've been having a good time, haven't we?
I believe friendship and sex can go together perfectly
well. I can't see why the befriended body should, by
definition, be excluded. We have warmth enough to go
round! Friendship is a deep-rooted and importunate
interest, but there is no need to fence anyone in. And
do stop staring at me like that. I have rather a lot on my
mind.

'She's thinking of Gasparino,' said Angelica Margherita heartlessly.

I said nothing, but I believed she was right. On that
wintry day in Naples I thought that was thinking, the
tight band of joy I could feel encircling my head. Before
my eyes I saw gestures, hands, lips, and not for a
moment did I ask myself whether the images were

retrospective, or perhaps betokened something that could start afresh any minute. How was I to know that when you are at the heart of a miracle, at the very epicentre, there can be no question of brain-work. You keep silent. Your breathing is shallow. You are, as if by magic, struck with myopia. Nothing must disturb your concentration. That thinking – I know now – would not start until later, once I was back on my husband's estate, once I was pregnant. The habit of sitting and thinking in the gloom overlooking the brilliantly lit stage of the San Carlo was to stay with me for the rest of my days. The love of my life had been a singer, and what I would cherish burnt into my brain until the day I died would consist of head notes, chest notes, changes in register, the laws of breathing and the angelic effrontery with which Gasparo, on the night of the première, had varied and embellished his arias. Everyone worshipped you, Gasparo, though the audience was left somewhat bemused that night, for there were no scowls, no mocking smiles, no belated entrances, there was none of that illustrious bad behaviour that tied in so delectably with our own, secret, faults.

By the way, I have taken the liberty of claiming your staggering display of virtuosity that night as a tribute to our love.

*

The Virtuoso

The opera we are hearing tonight is not new. Pergolesi's *Olimpiade* was performed several seasons ago in Rome, the twenty-five-year-old maestro was still alive then, and during the performance he sat at the cembalo to accompany the recitatives and to do some conducting. He was full of confidence. Working on this opera had been a love story, he had said, impetuous, blind and, as usual in matters of love, full of strange and paradoxical conquests. Besides, one afternoon during rehearsal a young poet had come up to him with tears in his eyes and had embraced him and kissed him on the mouth. The rest of the Roman audience, however, showed less appreciation. During the sinfonia they were attentively silent, but then there was a restiveness that passed into irritation, they turned their backs to the stage to chatter and shout, to gnaw at chickens and slurp wine, and Giambattista Pergolesi, in the last year of his life, was struck on the jaw by a small, overripe melon.

Naples adores him. Naples adores those arias of his that penetrate walls, the orchestrations that make you think of sun-drenched fields full of purple flowers. Naples, sobbing at the thought of the young composer's agony, knows she will enjoy his immortally fresh melodies tonight, rendered acceptable to the taste of our city, subtly modified and intensified by the incomparable Gasparino Conti, virtuoso.

It's a feast. The royal box is occupied by the king and

queen, the populace in the pit keep quiet. Gasparo sings his story in the flame-red glow of the exotic stage-set, we understand everything. He is a man, there is no doubt, and he is handsome. We lean forward, elbows on the parapet and want to get to know him on the self-evident condition: the voice is the person, not the sex. The world is the world of the performance.

Next to me sit Berto and the Sicilian. The profile of the latter is the work of gods. Forehead, nose, upper lip, chin. Berto and I are such good friends that yesterday he confided in me: 'I keep wanting to lie on top of him. His hips remind me of the flanks of a doe I shot and wounded once in the clumsiest possible way. He's fickle. His childhood was unhappy. If anyone so much as eyes him with disapproval I turn around like a fighting cock. I love his boasting, his injured feeling of self-respect, his petulant sulking, I sleep with the total devastation of his boyhood. My heart cringes. Even without taking his hand in mine, just when he sits beside me, I can feel the brevity of his life-line.'

Now their hands are entwined and resting next to mine on the plush-covered balustrade. The love duet, *Nei giorni tuoi felici*, which Gasparo is performing with remarkable courtesy, indeed tenderness, with the soprano Maria Mancini, is interpreted by my husband and his friend to suit their own randy inclinations. Lay your head on my shoulder ... brush the hair from my eyes . . . let us hold each other close in the tempest of life.

And everyone is doing the same thing. Everyone in this place is busy gleaning the precious ornaments with which Gasparo enhances the original music, for their own private hoard. The musical work of art: notation, throat, daydream. Everyone is in love and Gasparo just stands there, singing. Weak with desire, fetishistic, nymphomaniacal, we pick up his shakes and trills, embrace his fantasies and drag them, undaunted like beetles, like ants, over a dusty track in the forest, we push aside a heavy stone and let ourselves drop, clasping the gossamer filament, straight down into a darkness that by the second grows larger and wider.

Gasparo steps backwards, places his foot on an imitation rock and draws up his already thickening but still beautiful body. This singer is capable, when the fancy takes him, of magnificent acting. Tonight the expression on his face is exactly right for a prince who sets greater store by a friend's word of honour than by a lover's troth. We quiver. Now for the cadence.

People in love believe in infinity. People who aren't in love do the same. Why should we resign ourselves to misery? Common words fail us, and even cries, curses and sighs aren't good enough. The cadenza is a musical ornament that has to be sung in one breath just before the ritornello. Virtuosity: the ace soloist transcends the boundaries of form. A spray of distinct notes, acrobatic turns, cartwheels, saltos, of trills and diaphanous appoggiaturas soar into space. Now, for scores of seconds, a full minute, madness reigns. The capacities of life are ridiculed. A single breath becomes a whirlwind. We float to another universe, what pleasure, what lightness, we are driven mad with joy, yes, but let's be honest: surely not quite mad enough to forget our earthly fairy tales. Who has redeemed our hearts? By what caresses are we invisibly united? The only sensations you can take with you are those you have experienced yourself.

Gasparo! Here, in this theatre, I am surely the only one who buried my face in your armpit yesterday?

I listen to you. I follow a capricious series of notes swooping up to a cluster of *gruppetti*-above-the-note before cascading downwards and I am your slave like everyone else. But surely I am the only one to cast my mind back to the hair falling over your face yesterday, to the way you leaned on your forearms, tensed the muscles of your diaphragm while the movements of your white buttocks were doubled in the shadows of a Venetian looking-glass? I am jealous. You are everything to me. I listen along with everyone else to the complicated concluding series of trills and simply cannot bear the thought of anyone else in a dress of midnight-blue velvet standing by your bed, balancing the tip of one foot on the side, arching her neck like a heron stalking prey as she fastens the strap at her heel at the end of an afternoon that drifted past like a cloud.

The way I did, yesterday.

I had got up earlier than usual. I had put on a frock of midnight-blue velvet, low-necked, flounced. I had breakfasted, and jumped up. My desire for Gasparo, for sex, had driven me out of doors.

There is a difference between haste and impatience. Anyone in a hurry is short of time, you're a wretch who has to do everything more quickly than desirable. If you're impatient, though, you have minutes to spare. You want to speed up time and indicate to yourself how, for instance. Don't take a carriage. Run. Don't look straight ahead but look around and co-opt everything in that single interest: hurry! Concern yourself with as much as possible and before you know it you must make haste. I had agreed to meet my voluble darling before the midday hour.

Vaulted arches. Steps of porphyry. Brick-lined niches with birds huddling in their feathers. I arrived at the via Foria, picked my way between the puddles ringed with dried mud and crossed a square cluttered with market stalls for Christmas. Without slowing my pace I took in the black puddings, the plucked geese, the garlic meat, the mountains of lard decorated with gilt paper and the huge cheese-and-egg pies big enough to feed an entire family for a week.

'Where's your servant?' the pork butchers cried as I sped past, and I replied, truthfully, over my shoulder: 'Back there, following behind! A proud fellow with a shopping basket on his back!'

When I came upon the Donnaregina I could not resist stepping inside for a moment, this church was a refuge for miscreants on the run. I found them in a side chapel gathered in twos or threes playing cards, just one person was reading. I could smell clean linen, tobacco and, looking around, I noticed a pot of veal stew simmering on a wood-burning stove. I saw that Angelica Margherita's friend wasn't there any more, of course he wasn't, no one stayed here longer than the first flush of danger. A young man with gold wristbands offered me a glass of wine. Red or white? White, I said, because I had seen that one of the bottles cooling in the font was already open. We drifted into a conversation about Leibniz.

'Leibniz?' I cried. 'That's risky! What is your opinion of the soul without windows? We perceive nothing and give nothing. Our senses betray us, well, I don't know. Tra-tatata-tà ta ta . . . Please excuse me, there's a song that keeps going round in my head.'

And I put my glass down again, extended my fingers to my host, apologized anew and promised to come back.

Outside again. The grey winter's day. A beggar-woman in the church square, I have no time. I have no time and anyway, where's my purse? I offered the

woman alms that made her eyes flash: 'May the Holy
Virgin protect you.' I hurried on.

In the via Armeno I had to push my way past the
Nativity scenes, there were too many cribs to count, on
trestles, on the ground, people carried them in their
arms or hugged them to their chests, the very best
handwork, Signora, I'm not joking, such a lovely little
group, the most adorable baby, an ass, an ox, do stop
and look! Is there anything as undermining to civil
conduct as sex?

From a tavern came guitar music. Turkish slave-girls
offered me coffee, with honeyed smiles. A small fire was
burning on a balcony. Where was I? I stopped to get my
breath back at a house where a Madonna, lonely and
forlorn, stood immured in the façade. No flowers, no
lanterns, she drew my supplicant attention.

'Queen of the sea! Golden house! May this afternoon
for once not go by in a god-forsaken flash!'

She drew up her shoulders, shivering. She coughed.
'All right, all right, you silly thing, I'll slow things down
a little.'

I arrived at the house on the via San Carlo to find
Gasparo seated at the harpsichord. Out of breath, I laid
my cold cheek against his face. He carried on playing.
My hand under his armpit. He kept his eyes fixed on
the music in front of him. Along the chain of his watch,
his leather belt, his thigh muscles which contracted each
time he moved his feet, his groin. He turned a page and

drummed on. My infatuated hands crossed the path of Girolamo Frescobaldi's toccata in G minor. Gentle pressure, rubbing, cheeky little nudges and a piece of music that, after a lazy start, soon makes extraordinary demands on the thumb – that most important of fingers which imposes its will on the rest of the hand – on the timely lifting of the individual fingers and on the lower arms which it is best to hold in a position slightly lower than the keyboard.

*

I had gone to the window. Behind my back the city turning grey in the December sky. Ahead of me a door with gilt panels. In between, a celebrated man playing a harpsichord for just one, privileged listener: me. Life is beautiful.

Am I in love with your fame? Am I usurping your applause each time I kiss you?

I melted at the sight of his busy hands, his hunched shoulders, his face of which I had a full view, heavy eyelids, grave expression, yes, it was especially the gravity that threw me. When silence fell, the piece having come to an end, he graced me with a glance – by way of concession, it should be noted, for he promptly turned to a fresh page and focused his attention on a point miles away from me.

These singers did more than train their voices in their schooldays. They are masters on the harpsichord, often on the violin too. Sealed off from the outside world on the top floor of the *conservatorio* they spent interminable hours studying counterpoint and composition. Hand those students a libretto, pick a date, and they will duly come up with an effortless score for *The Martyrdom of San Gennaro,* a music drama in three acts.

He had played Scarlatti, he had played Van Wassenaer, he had briefly put his hands on his neck, looked up at the ceiling, and then he had sung for me such a strange-sounding, compelling *Stabat Mater* that my soul was set ablaze like parched grassland, my feet left the ground. You are a demon, an angel, this is witchery. You know, don't you, that you are not one of us mortals . . . ?

Then he looked at me. He no longer sang but talked, standing close to me. Emerging from a radiant echo I heard the door open. An old man came in, knelt by the hearth and poked the fire. There was the distant clatter of plates, lids, dishes. Gasparo said: '. . . because, you see, these modern pieces are often written down in a great hurry. Although I must say it suits me fine. What you get is just a rough sketch and it's up to you to draw out the cadence from the actual notation, the movement which is implicitly understood, the natural pulse, the, the . . .' – he was groping for the right word, snapped his fingers – 'the *swing.*'

'I'm listening,' I said softly, quite contented still. 'Tell me how you do it.'

For I began to realize that you can take hold of a dream between forefinger and thumb and turn it over to see what's on the other side. Technique. Mundane tricks of the trade. He went over to the table where a carafe of white Cyprus wine stood prepared and he explained earnestly that in order to cut the aria loose from the notes it is necessary to improvise and embellish. 'The only way for a beginner to learn is by listening to an expert.'

He loosened his tie.

'It's such fun to force a triple time into double in such a way that you still keep the division of three beats.'

What? I almost laughed. Not at his words, but at his expression, which showed exactly the same emotion – I swear it was so – as a Dutchman discussing bulbs. Oh the purity of craftsmanship! And the language of the craft! The lingua franca of sharps and flats or, equally, of soil types, crops, weather conditions. There exists a very rare tulip known by the name of Admiral van Hoorn.

Tell me, kind sir, where exactly do you come from? someone had asked the blushing baron last Saturday, in our crowded salon. He had replied dutifully: from a country estate by the sea where, in the month of April, brilliantly coloured fields reach as far as the eye can see. And what about that obsession of your people, those blooms? He told us that where he came from the soil consists of sand mixed with clay, and that the groundwater is kept at a very high level, which is easy enough because the entire country is criss-crossed with ditches and canals which are all, without exception, controlled by sluices and pumping installations. Look, I'll draw you a diagram, the water reaches up to here, just under the bulb, and that's why we're able to force the bloom before it's naturally due, and so . . . In short, everyone listened open-mouthed to the young Dutchman whose eyes seemed to emit beams of bright yellow, blue and red.

Tell me how you do it.

Three in the afternoon and we had finished our meal. Again we had withdrawn to the small glistening chamber filled with the deepening yellow glow of candle-light. We had talked about musical ornaments at table.

'They cover profundity with roses,' Gasparo had said.

'Yes,' I had replied. 'They fly about a greasy neck on angel's wings.'

'Some more?'

'Oh yes, please.'

'Red or white?'

'Red.'

Tell me how you do it . . . in heaven's name tell me how you manage to sing for such an unspeakably long time without taking a breath, I muttered, half in exasperation, but first put your arms around me. Massage my neck and cheeks with your plump, ever pouty lips and then tell me all about virtuosity being the same as virtue, I will not disagree. Again our shoes lay strewn across the floor. We drank from the same glass. Gasparo stretched, yawning, and I knew what this signified: I'm getting in the mood. That afternoon everything was just right. Music, table conversation and food had been reduced to the most simple yet ardent and compelling gestures. Lift my skirt. Let your hands trace a network of delicate ornaments around my hips and other regions. Can you see why life without you is unthinkable? You are the adventure that happens only once in a lifetime. It is winter. The birds are deserting the city but my bones are suffused with a light, sunny, definitive warmth. Isn't bliss the ultimate proof of the existence of a Creator who thus, through our pleasure, wishes to be adored? I know it pleases men when you place your hand without further ado on their flies.

'All right then, come along, you're always so cheerful,' he said, and he was ready to lie down on the bed with me.

Gasparo was the kind of person who required some persuasion in the area of love. His reticence was not only due to his physical status, also his soul took some rousing. He was inclined to dismiss everything outside his specialism as somewhat peculiar. Yet sometimes he had such a dreamy look in his eyes during my efforts at seduction that my passion was instantly doubled. Cling to me, relax, I'll spread my legs wide, let yourself go and in the meantime feel free to scrutinize my shining cheeks and open mouth. This is the most dignified expression I can muster. Go ahead and compare all of this, in your unconscious thoughts, with for instance the *Mare infido agitata*, the aria in which the voice carries on without breathing for twenty terrible bars in a nerve-racking tempo, attacking a complex of trills and great swoops in imitation of the gathering storm, sea and shipwreck which, as everyone knows, is madness, acrobatic vocalism, half-witted ecstasy that taunts the laws of aesthetics.

I love you. You are a dry river. I wade through you and through a landscape without end. That the laws of procreation do not apply for once suits me very well. There will be no need to implore St Monica nor to have recourse to my chambermaid's vinegar bottle.

A kingdom by the sea. A city. A theatre where the harpsichords are being tuned already. Gasparo was a man with a beautiful body and a warm mouth. His climax was shallow. At the zenith of love he held his breath for a moment, all I felt inside me was a brief, slight tremor, a sigh beside my ear. Nebulous satisfaction. There was no seed. No moisture, apart from mine. They call that a dry run, I told him. The term, which I had learnt from my French lover, was new to him.

*

'How many of you slept there? Sixteen? Sixteen young castrati?'

He had been dozing in my arms and had woken up when I wriggled my hand, which was turning numb, from under him. What was it like to live in the *conservatorio*, I had asked. The only ones in that draughty orphanage to have a decent bed, I've heard, were the little singers, because of their market value: in an Easter procession those lads can easily raise twenty ducats.

He glanced at me, tranquil, awake but still a little weak.

'We called ourselves eunuchs,' he said. And the stories about draughty halls and hardship were exaggerated.

The building looked grim. A cedar growing in the courtyard took all the sun away. Although the rules prescribed quiet and discipline, there were always quick-footed lads in dingy white cassocks scampering up and down the corridors and staircases. Haste and noise, forbidden games, forbidden bullying, the harsh time-table was crammed with music classes as well as lessons in rhetoric, grammar, the classics. Gasparo was one of the élite, but also the common boarders whose genitals were intact were not recruited from the slums. The bell rang at sunrise, the children jumped straight out of bed and the young choristers on the top floor did so to the accompaniment of a loud, shrill song that made every-one's blood curdle for miles around. *Laudate Dominum* at five in the morning, Gasparo poked his head and arms into a worn surplice and smoothed the folds. He looked pale. Still half asleep he went to chapel, quickly joined in the mass which was not supposed to exceed twenty minutes and descended among hundreds of other boys to the refectory where on some days there was sufficient bread and even luke-warm gruel. He ate quickly, taking no notice of anyone, his thoughts already filled with the runs and scales he was about to practise and the scores that boys like him could read without thinking, simply like a book: black signs are colourful facts.

It's amazing how someone else's stories can nestle in your head. I glanced at his face from time to time as he spoke and couldn't quite read his expression. But when he said: 'My singing master had the patience of a devil,' I had a very clear picture of a lonely, worn-out Gasparino in the terrifying presence of a man who was a tutor, foster father, master and above all a tyrant.

'Why don't we pull up the blanket?' I mumbled.

But Gasparo wasn't cold at all. He said: 'Look, I was his best pupil and so he was strict. There were lessons about the mechanics of the voice but also about nerve and sang-froid, because having him glaring at you with his neck sticking out stiff as a rod, when you stood in the classroom singing the same slowly rising scale for the thousandth time, could make you feel very peculiar. Well, I could handle that, also because I realized early on that his method was crafty. Diatonic and chromatic scales, sequences of thirds, fourths, fifths, trills and

turns in simple groups: that he had deconstructed singing into its most basic components was a clever inven-
tion, but what I thought and still think was really
brilliant, let me tell you, was what he said about
breathing. To say that singing depends on respiration is
true but it's also a truism, because we all know that life
itself is nothing but breathing. So why should a singer
have to work so hard at it? Tensing the buttocks,
expanding the rib-cage, tilting the pelvis? My teacher
was an outrageous character who loved turning things
upside down and then being proved right. It's the
singing that develops the breathing and not the breathing the singing.'

He paused, nodded emphatically and repeated: 'Singing invokes breathing, not the other way round.'

He had lived there for seven years. Between eleven
and eighteen Gasparo endured a life of subordination
and harsh discipline in a run-down building. He did not
suffer, he simply grew up, and he never wondered
whether he was wasting his youth. When he stood
practising in that overcrowded college, where in the
auditorium the instrumentalists vied with each other at
top speed, and the singers on the upper floors and in the
corridors started out *sotto voce* but gradually, via a
terrible insidious crescendo, decided it was time to make
themselves heard and many of them just started yelling,
when Gasparo, in that bedlam, executed his transparent
vocalises, he knew himself to be master of his own fate.

He was not distracted by the pandemonium nor by the bluebottles buzzing around his head, because he understood that he was the best singer on earth and if anyone had asked him at the time whether he didn't feel that love was the most important thing in life, he would have looked up in surprise. Naturally. Yet that is exactly how I feel. All that matters is what you can achieve with tenderness, strength and irresistible beauty.

'Dear God,' he muttered, 'that stench in winter at about six in the evening, when it rained and down below in the kitchens they prepared tripe with garlic. Do you think they allowed even one window to be opened?'

'But Gasparo,' I said. 'It was a prison, you were a prisoner.'

I knew that wasn't entirely true. The little singers made regular excursions into the city. Even then they were in demand to sing during mass, they had their fixed part to play in the blood processions and they rode in the flower-bedecked floats in honour of the Virgin Mary, raising their razor-sharp voices to whip the devotion of thousands upon thousands of people into an emotional apotheosis smothered in tears and sobs: 'Long live God!' The churches squabble over the boys' voices. The schooled children sing in all the sanctuaries of Naples and beyond, and they participate, in the name of God and the martyrs, in the madcap comedies that are habitually performed at Christmas and Easter in the monasteries of Capua, Monte Cassino and the island of

Capri. Most of all, however, they are indispensable in the presence of death.

Gasparo would always remember his first wake. He had not been summoned. Twenty-year-old Nina Di Majo's widower had asked for four boys, Gasparo had not been chosen. After supper, following an urge he could not define, he went to the dormitory in the attic where the four boys were changing their clothes. It was August and a heavy heat still lingered in the air. He wet his hair in front of the mirror, wiped his face, went over to the wardrobe with the rows of white cassocks and surplices, all clean and tidy, and sank down on a knee over the shiny buckle of his shoe. Then he turned round to face the other boys, and addressed the one who looked a bit of a dunce.

'What are you going to sing tonight?' he asked, tensely.

'The *Lux aeternam*. The *Pie Jesu*. The *Ave verum*.'

'I'll bribe you. Let me take your place.'

The boy looked with respect and silent refusal at the brass coins Gasparo held out to him.

Thereupon Gasparo decided to climb out of a window on the floor below, and to slide down a warm wall covered in lizard-cracks into the still, moonlit night which, for the duration of the vigil, would be spent a few streets away, in a house with a hundred windows.

V

The young woman was beautifully laid out. They had dressed her in red and put artificial flowers in her hair, which they had draped over her shoulders and breast, very black, shiny, still growing quietly down her neck. For a moment upon entering Gasparo thought the dead woman was looking at him, greeting him with a kind of horror: on each eyelid lay a gold Virgin Mary scapular, and the metal flashed on and off with the light reflected from the tapers burning behind her head.

It had been easy to become a participant in this vigil. As soon as the heavy door swung open Gasparo had quickly joined the other boys and burst into song with them. His gaze was unswerving as he advanced through a colonnaded hall. He felt a hand on his head. 'Well done,' a pair of lips murmured by his ear. Everyone was glad to see the boys. Healthy people in splendid clothes kept smiling wide and showed them the way. There, straight ahead, yes, my goodness aren't they adorable, how beautifully they sing, over there, beyond the balustrade and the pearl-grey curtains, why boys, what's this tune you're singing? To be sure, your rapid recitation of the eulogy will not break a sorrowful silence in this grand hall designed for festivities and balls, it will interrupt the low-voiced hubbub of a multitude of friends and relations gathered around a young husband with limpid eyes and dressed in purple, cracking his knuckles one by one.

'Would you like a raisin sorbet or do you prefer lemon?'

The night was warm. Midges danced in the open windows. Gasparo felt surrounded by mindlessness, he was not at all bothered. The people were mourning. The weak feeling in their stomachs was not a sign of grief, but something else. All eyes were drawn to the illuminated spot in the centre of the hall where Nina, fresh and silent in her death, lay supine. Five boys sat on folding chairs at her feet. It was an outing for them. They looked around with a self-possessed air, nudged each other when it was time to get up and sing and were offered refreshments after each hymn, each series of canzonette.

'Hello there, what's wrong? Don't you like the cake?'

Gasparo looked up. It was the widower offering him a wafer-thin folded pancake filled with tomato and rosemary.

No one wept. The mourners, heavy-hearted, drank

gratefully and now and then stepped forward magnanimously to take a closer look. 'How lovely she looks!' But most of them were thinking: Farewell dearest, we loved you, and now you are gone. Your eyes are closed, your lips too, your senses are a walled fortress, you have lost the ability to smell. We are awed, none the less, by the icy reverie behind your forehead, so we will not take to our beds tonight. No darkness for us. Cupboards will remain cupboards and tables tables. This house, five storeys high, remains firmly standing. Can you hear the boys? We sent for them to cheer you up. What good can our tears do? *Salve regina coelorum*, dear God the beauty of it. Their voices, shimmering and darting like butterflies, are conversing with your soul. While you move away from us and from the pastures of this earth, they will accompany you a little way, towards the mist, the sunless atmosphere.

Gasparo was staring. He was tipping his chair and staring at a girl who would never age, whose beauty would never fade.

White throat, white hands.

And the last vestiges of hearing.

What was the cold under her dress to him?

*

Figlioli, little sons, is what they are called, the precious boys who still resemble ordinary lads although they are already different. A church door swings open, a mass for the dead is under way, a dais hung with purple, gold and white is mounted by a row of little milksops, what are they thinking? One day their dreams, the dreams every child inherits from its mother's womb, are violently disrupted, yet nothing has been taken away from them. They enjoy performing and their little tunics suit them to perfection. A grossly overweight prelate makes way for them. Clerics of the lower ranks take their places along the sides of the priests' choir, silence. For a moment the congregation don't know what to do, they stare in silence at the coffin in front of the altar, wreathed in incense. Then it's *their* turn, the boys from the orphanage. Brazenly they intercede in the dialogue between heaven and earth and, yes, the opposite poles of life and afterlife do seem to approach one another. *From the depths of despair I beseech thee, Oh Lord . . . Hear my prayer . . .* To the question as to the meaning of life they open, with a most resolute expression, their mouths. Ancient phrases begin to swirl and jostle in a strange, melodic way, our hearts rejoice, *figlioli*, gift from heaven. Between the world of men and the kingdom of God exist the warmest of relations.

Just about all our great singers began their careers in church. It's fun to be an angel. Just as it's fun, a few years on, to be a woman.

For that is the order of rank: first angel, then woman.

*

His costume had been laid out for him. It was the robe of the Queen of Carthage and everyone in the dressing room agreed that it was a veritable work of art.

Gasparo turned up just before eight. He was attended by his singing master and a young *abate*, both men having accompanied him on his journey from Naples. Without uttering a word he went straight to the costume to inspect the silk and muslin and run his fingers along the gold-embroidered billowing skirt, the waist was very narrow.

'The measurements are exactly right,' said one of the dressers.

Gasparo nodded but still did not speak. He had just turned eighteen. A bashful, strapping youth, with a soft, almost mature body. He was so beautiful that whoever set eyes on him for the first time stopped and stared in amazement. But there was a certain bluntness about his beauty. It had the unfathomable bluntness of a young person who has never felt the blood boil. How on earth could he have discovered the wonders of his being and his gender? Until recently all his days had been so alike that now, in retrospect, he perceived them as one and the same rapidly executed musical scale. One morning a few months ago his singing master had looked him up and down with a smile of tender emotion and had said: 'I have taught you all I know.' Then came the invitation to make his stage début at the Teatro delle Dame in Rome.

Someone touched him.

'Go on, get a move on. The performance begins in an hour and a half.'

He did not respond.

'Where's the wig?' he mumbled.

'Here,' someone said behind him. 'Take a look, I'm sure you'll like it.'

He turned and saw a wig-stand crowned by a towering structure of silvery-white curls decorated with blood-red ribbons and tiny moonbirds nestling in little hollows. The maids eyed him with maternal solicitude. 'And here's your train, here the fan and the bracelets. In a moment you will be the most beautiful woman in the world.'

Gasparo blushed. 'All right,' he said. 'Where can I hang my coat?'

The room was a warm, airless cavern. Amongst the brass-framed mirrors hung the heavy aroma of candles, wax flowers, ironing, greasepaint and all sorts of people in various states of agitation. How would this carefully nurtured talent perform? He was so curiously calm, so earnest, so grave. Did he not know that the Roman public was notorious for its teasing? Whispering faces peered round the door. The news that a country bumpkin with an uncommonly pretty face was to be thrown to the lions tonight had spread quickly through the theatre. Everyone wanted a glimpse of what they were doing to him.

The singer was stripped of his clothing down to his underwear, and the fumbling hands did not stop there. The drawstring was loosened, the pants slid down, the body of Gasparo, pale and smooth like that of a young pig, was observed with interest.

'Angel! Treasure!' someone sighed behind the door. 'You needn't even open your mouth for me!'

Now for the stockings, raise your foot, young man, lean on my shoulder, is the elastic too tight? A corset was wrapped around him from behind, that's just right, pull hard on those laces and see the delightful pair of half-naked breasts burgeoning from the bodice!

The singing master looked anxious.

'Not too tight, for God's sake!' he protested.

'But there's room for another two fingers at least,' one of the maids retorted.

The singing master mopped the perspiration from his neck. 'Take a deep breath now,' he instructed the best pupil he had ever had and would ever have.

Blue eye shadow, black kohl, pearl-pink powder, Gasparo's wavy chestnut hair was tied together between his shoulder blades. Stepping carefully into his costume there was a ringing in his ears. The wig was lifted on to his head. Time to breathe.

A cry sounded in the doorway.

'Come and look! He's prettier than a real woman!'

From somewhere came the sound of a harpsichord.

Gasparo went over to the mirror and opened his eyes

wide. He stood, motionless: Didone, queen of Carthage, tangible and within reach, the corners of the mouth upturned. He no longer felt a stranger.

'There you are, dear boy,' a maid's voice said behind him. 'A first-rate lady, can you believe it? So what do you think?'

His lips moved fractionally.

'Thank you, very nice.'

The harpsichord fell silent. From the corner of his eye he saw his singing master loom towards him, craning his neck and staring at him intently.

'Excellent. There will be coffee later, but come along with me. The audience are already taking their seats. Now is the time when it's essential for you to warm up your voice.'

He leaned back to take a final look in the mirror and was satisfied with his sanguine, imperturbable reflection. 'But you see ...' he muttered, addressing no one in particular. Then he reached for his fan and gave a small laugh as he led the way into the adjoining room where the harpsichord stood.

'Gasparo.'

His singing master awaited him anxiously.

Then Gasparo sang a series of triples, coolly and firmly, his voice steadily gathering brilliance as the time drew near and the boxes filled up with people shrugging their shoulders and wondering: 'D'you suppose he'll be any good, this new fellow?'

It was just before ten o'clock when he made his entrance. The overture and the first aria had come and gone and the applause for the *primo uomo* went on and on. Gasparo took his time. Drained, feeling as if a wall was being pushed aside, he stepped forward. He stared into the pitch-black auditorium, heard the lost sound of a violin and sensed in the depths of his soul that he was alive.

A tense silence had fallen.

*

Dazzlement. Rome looked at a woman.

Women have resplendent bodies that exude euphoria. They have bellies like tables, breasts like divans, shoulders like windowsills catching the rays of the sun and their skin is more resilient than a cushion of moss fringed with flowers. Women in Rome are clandestine merchandise, they are strictly forbidden to appear on stage.

The illusion was perfect. During the prelude to the aria Gasparo, waiting for his cue, strolled across the stage and glanced indolently up at the boxes. The look in his eyes set every heart ablaze, male and female alike. Goddess! Is it really me you are looking at? We worship your beauty which will never grow angular or hard, your skin will never be stubbled. The beauty of a woman surpasses that of a man in every sense!

Since women know exactly how far they can go, they also know how to undermine all sense of propriety and so enchant anyone they fancy. The Papal State does not permit women to sing, play music, or act, and according to Innocent XIII their low-cut French gowns ought to be washed and ironed too hot in the laundries. Is it not so, ladies? Your smile is a gateway, your gaze a corridor, your embrace a summer patio with a sparkling fountain, so lock up your rooms. Let no one in, least of all the music teacher.

Gasparo breathed in and out resolutely. His manner, quite unintentionally, expressed great sensuality. As the orchestral introduction came to an end the audience watched him turn graciously to his partner, the celebrated soprano Giovanni Di Caro in the role of Enea. The supercilious smile on the face of the man advancing towards him did not appear to disturb Gasparo in the least, perhaps he didn't even notice. He spread his fan and stretched out his white arms to the audience.

Rome. City of abstract reason where small and weak things are treated as if they did not exist. It may seem odd, but a majestic corpus of logic and order feels threatened by three entities that count as insatiable. Earth. Hell. The female sexual organs. Women have little blood, their legs are feeble and their skulls lamentably brittle. That their corpses float on their backs in water is bad enough, but far more exasperating is the weakness of their intellect which esteems a beautiful poem more highly than dogma. Rome, worldly city of drama and love, what strikes the visitor most in the streets, theatres, palaces?

The women. What makes Rome so charming is the abundance of women enveloped in velvet and lace strolling in the streets. Where on earth do they all come from? At balls and masquerades it is quite common to see the young, sophisticated lady of the house holding out her hand to be kissed by a maidservant – a maidservant in daring and elegant attire, true, but also with scrupulously shaven cheeks that are tainted, as the evening wears on, with a bluish haze. Could that be Bonifacio Bozzi the patrician? Certainly, and that slim, straight-backed officer is Count Luca's daughter. Lackeys in breeches and waistcoats wait on clusters of boyish girls wearing tartan hunting skirts. Everyone jumps up at the opening bars of a minuet. It is instructive and amusing to exchange your sex for another in the closet from time to time.

Everyone sat up straight. The three final chords rang out, some people in the audience rubbed their eyes to make sure that everything they were about to see was true. They watched the débutant as he raised his eyes and lowered them again. He was concentrating. He was on the point of taking a deep breath when Giovanni Di Caro, his celebrated partner, suddenly addressed him. The ensuing dialogue could only be heard by the occupants of the boxes closest to the stage.

'Where exactly do you come from?' asked Di Caro.

'From Naples,' Gasparo replied, taken aback.

'Who's your patron saint?'

'The Holy Virgin, and the Siren too.'

The first singer gave him a leisurely, honeyed smile.

'D'you know what I like about you?' he said. 'Your face, with which you'll be singing all those false notes later on.'

Gasparo glanced at him thoughtfully, said nothing and then turned fully towards the hungry expectation of the dark house. The A on which the queen of Carthage begins her age-old lament was the longest and purest he had ever sung.

Then everyone stopped thinking their thoughts. They were unaware of their own smiles and many of them could hardly believe that time was flowing on and that at some point death would be waiting for them. The song fell on unusually generous hearts. All the animosity drained away now that they were feasting on the voice and the radiance of a lover who was not a woman but something far more convincing, the personification of woman.

However there was one person in the house who was in a vile temper, filled with disquiet about his reputation.

'Now for the duet,' said Giovanni Di Caro when the cheering subsided. 'Let's see if you can keep up with me.'

And keep up he did. Proudly erect, Didone stood facing her lover. Three feet and an ocean of hostility divided them. The hero filled the house with a tangle of vocal ornaments, like closely wrought wire, in a tempo that made a mockery of human reality. His partner responded with the facility of fluff in a breeze. An upward swoop like a flash of sulphur was countered by a casual turn, an absolutely ridiculous modulation was picked up and rendered acceptable, yet a vibrant crescendo was returned by a shower of trills, finer than stardust: as it happened, the two singers were beginning to enjoy themselves.

During the orchestral intermezzo Di Caro clamped his plumed helmet more firmly on his skull and then nodded meaningfully at his partner.

'So far so good,' he called, his voice rising above the violins.

Gasparo's reaction was cool.

'We haven't finished yet.'

'I say,' shouted Di Caro, 'You're not bad at all. What are they paying you?'

'Thirty *zecchini* and . . .' – Gasparo hesitated – '. . . and a genuine tortoiseshell snuffbox.'

Di Caro took a few steps forward and pressed his young colleague warmly to his chest. 'Well, well, what a bunch a skinflints! You're worth more than ten times as much!'

Then the consonance started for real. The legendary lovers' duet is performed by two men. Their instincts have been sidetracked. Their voices are high. Yet the

ears of the entranced audience know that these are not
the voices of women. It's not the number of vibrations
that resonates, it's a body, your body is what you are.
The timbre of the boyish voice, and the supple larynx of
the woman, and the strength and the size of the male
organ: the language of a pair of mythological lovers is
not commonplace. And their sex life is no ordinary
matter either.

Dissonant seconds. Downward and upward movements, small clashes. From the darkness the audience
looked towards a glass world bathed in rosy light. The
two high-pitched voices were indistinguishable and distinct by turns, they were also united from time to time.
The interval that is no longer an interval but twice the
same tone is known as a prime. It is called pure. Quite
conceivable that immaculate love exists. In the house,
where the temperature rose as time went on and the
floor became littered with the evil-smelling detritus of a
gala event, sat two young women. They were friends
and wore very pretty party dresses and were both
considerably younger than their husbands.

*

You were invited by the girls. The sensation of the
season, an incomprehensible and unsullied talent,
received the usual tokens of admiration. You sat
comfortably in a calash, elbows on your knees, and read
the note that had been slipped to you in the commotion

following the performance yesterday. You were curious, the address was near the Quirinal, you recalled the two smiling mouths perfectly well, and the little sign made by a handkerchief so ostentatiously dropped at your feet – that hunchbacked driver might as well hurry up as far as you were concerned. Your route took you along the Aurelian Wall, then to the bend in the Tiber. Since it had been raining for days the whole neighbourhood was flooded, the swines rooted contentedly in the mire, you yawned, whistled between your teeth, above the Forum the sun suddenly broke through the clouds. Dereliction, weeds and more cattle, it was market day. Between the arches from antiquity stood cows, you saw a man with two hens hanging by their feet from his belt perched on a post, the neck of a Doric column projecting from the earth. By a half-buried arch built by Septimius Severus shoppers crowded around a kettle of boiling meat. Then you arrived. It was a palace constructed of blocks of stone reclaimed from the Colosseum. 'The ladies are upstairs,' the maid told you. You looked up and saw a staircase lined with reliefs of early Christian sarcophagi.

'You look lovely,' Giulia said after a while, 'but we have to get used to you like this. We know you in your other clothes.'

You were given a warm welcome. On the couch by the fire, across the bed in the corner and a glimpse of soft cushions through a slit in the curtains, you could feel that the rules of conduct were relaxed in this place. There was nothing to stop you from making yourself at home and taking off your wig. The girls looked happy, we are dying of thirst they said, and they walked about in bare feet. When the flaxen-haired Francesca reached you a glass, you saw a thread of gold in her unblinking eyes.

'Look!' said Giulia by the windows.

You went over to her side in your white silk shirt, straight, your feet planted slightly apart so that you looked like a glorified deck-hand, and when you followed her gaze and discovered the piper in the street below taking up position with a solemn air at the foot of a statue of the Virgin, she put her arm around your waist.

'Actually it's a statue of Juno,' she said.

'Oh,' you replied. 'Doesn't he know?'

'He doesn't care in the least, he hasn't cared for days. He's playing a novena. He makes plenty of money.'

At that point the melody started. You were taken aback by the soft, warm frolic of another tongue in your mouth.

Francesca, Giulia and you dined at the table with the candelabra. In some mysterious way you had become close in a very short time. Besides, the sky darkened outside and the wind started blowing. 'Nothing better than lying in bed with a storm raging outside,' said Francesca. She turned to you and Giulia with a faraway look, lowered her eyes, stretched a little and knocked over her wine. 'Lend me your napkin, will you,' she said apologetically. And you handed her the napkin and said: 'No, nothing better.' Then the three of you crept into bed, like young hounds, and the curtains ballooned and fell to. The room would have seemed suddenly deserted had it not been for that corner of laughter and murmuring and the kind of purposeful rustling sound you make when you crouch on the forest floor in summer to gather moist scarlet strawberries, which you gulp down by the handful.

'This, and this, and this . . .' the two friends whispered. 'This is what we wanted to do from the moment we saw you.' Whereupon you heaved an ear-splitting sigh to indicate that, for all you cared, the world could go on turning.

When the three of you re-emerged, you rang for coffee. You buttoned up your clothes, sat down at the table and started making animal noises to see who was most convincing.

*

He triumphed. During the whole season Gasparo Conti, all prettied up and with roses in his hair, trod the boards in Rome. He was fondly referred to as Gasparino. The young soprano revelled in his new-found power. He who had exchanged the sun and the blue sky of his childhood for singing lessons was following his second nature, which was aimed not at conquest but at enchantment, not at warmth but at recognition. And he soon realized that there was no need to step aside for any mortal.

One evening in January – they were doing Porpora's *Semiramide* – a fellow singer, a tenor to boot, had already irritated him backstage by getting in his way more than once. When the man embarked on his aria too early by mistake, something occurred to Gasparo: my dear fellow, your face doesn't appeal to me. Not your face and not your voice either. Why do you bellow like that? And why, all the while, that look as though you're performing miracles? Don't you realize that by taking the octave in that crazy chest voice you've ruined my light *sotto voce* even before I've begun? Then, vexed as he was, Gasparo walked to the front and crowed like a cock, miaowed, and to amuse the audience for as long as it took his colleague to finish, did a series of bird imitations, among which the nightingale received the most applause.

'We were in stitches!' Francesca and Giulia said the next day.

He stared at them sheepishly and did not join in their laughter, he hadn't even done it for fun.

Throughout the winter dance bands played in the old houses with the blue ceilings. Gasparo was expected everywhere. As soon as he arrived he always looked round to see if his girlfriends were there. If they were not he would leave, or he would submit off-handedly, and wearing a vague expression, to the attentions of his doting admirers. On one of those grand evenings a high-ranking ecclesiastic, a cardinal although he was young still and good-looking, lavished such heart-rending attention on him that his world suddenly narrowed. The ballroom, the orchestra and the other guests faded from his vision: Gasparo gazed into the moist depths of two black pupils. A hand pressed his hand, a knee touched his knee, he sat on the edge of his chair and to his own surprise launched into a glowing description of the farewell scene in the *Didone*, of her last steps, when she carries herself forward at the inevitably reduced tempo of a three-four time towards the burning city of Carthage '... and then the orchestra plays unisono, you know what I mean, those eighths, first C, then D flat then B flat, and then I come in with: I go ... but where do I go ...? and then switch unnoticed from twelve-eight to three-four, and now you think, as well you might, what's the difference, triple time is triple time, but precisely because the preceding recitative is in common time you can be sure you'll get that peculiar ... Anyway, all I'm trying to say is that I'm glad the final scene is my monologue – which is highly unusual as it happens, although it was already done in the *Arsace* ...'

He was rewarded with a delighted smile, it was late already, carriages were waiting in the dark wintry night. In papal Rome it was inadvisable for a cardinal to dine with a woman, but surely no one could object to a castrated boy. Gasparo had spent all evening singing, but he did not feel tired in the least. In a while, flushed with pleasant conversation, he would go home with someone.

He pouted.

'But next season I want to sing the male lead.'

And so it occurred. Upon Gasparo's return to Rome after a summer of touring and guest performances it was the Teatro Argentina that insisted on engaging him. The negotiations in the impresario's office were agreeable. A fee, his own home, servants and a carriage, what more could you want? Quite frankly: the following. Still tanned by the sun, a tumbler of coffee in his hand, Gasparo stood his ground. In Venice he had been Aminta, in Turin Ariadne. This winter in Rome he would be Nero.

Première in the Teatro Argentina in Rome. The audience settled in their seats with mixed feelings about what to expect. Gasparo entered in a triumphal horse-drawn chariot. The most portentous character in opera is still the hero in boots and tight breeches. He drew his sabre. The noise died away at once. Hesitation. A tender cantabile in the orchestra. Uproarious laughter rose from the pit, only to be taken up in the galleries and greeted by whistles in the gods. There was jeering and shouting to Get Lost.

INTERMEZZO

Faustina Maria Delle Papozze is old. One more day, alas, and death will take her, she is quite unaware. In the early-morning light, on her way from the house to the stables, she walks down a lane lined with blossoming hawthorn on a country estate at Altavilla. The day promises to be glorious. Faustina, bent and with age-spotted face, thinks vaguely of other mornings like this one, in the old days, mornings in May when the low red sun already full of warmth banishes the low-lying mists from the charmed landscape in that early hour. Goodness me, what radiant light!

A row of cypresses separates the stables from the orchard. Aah, she kneels on the ground by the stable door. Using both hands she tugs at the bottom edge of the wood. This little old woman, quite enterprising still in her maid's smock, has today for the first time since winter been liberated from the feeling of approaching death.

'And you just won't budge, will you?' she grumbles at the door. 'What's got into you?'

At last the door gives way to admit Faustina into the dank and gloomy space so that she can untie the dear creature in the corner by the manger and lead him outside.

'Cicotto, it's me.'

The animal has already pricked up his grey ears in her direction. Cicotto is a sixteen-year-old thorough-bred, capable of finding the way to Naples, three days' journey away, without any guidance.

An old woman is an old woman, and a horse a horse. How can those two creatures have got the very same notion into their heads? There they stand in the fresh morning air, serene, complacent like two scholars who have arrived at some conclusion concerning the universe. Dogs bark down in the valley. The curved sweep of mountains is sprinkled with houses. Faustina rose this morning with a dry, sweet smell in her nose. Hey, just a moment . . . In a flash of breathtaking lucidity she decided to return for ever to the city where she was born so precipitously one September day in 1681.

Precipitously, Madonna, holy little slave-mother, you can say that again! In a basement dwelling behind the piazza Selleria a swollen woman lifts up her skirt because she feels something odd. The pressure inside her body, familiar and heavy, has suddenly shifted. There, that's sensible. In a shaft of daylight falling in through the door, it occurs to Faustina's mother-to-be to squat and clasp her hands like a bowl under her bulging belly. Beppo!

The man lying by the sooty wall is wide awake at once. He realizes he must get out of bed, and, with a gesture of infinite care, take over the small burden his wife will hand over to him. She has let herself go now and screams, rolls her eyes, aaa . . . aaa . . .! The whole neighbourhood cannot help hearing. Then a bunch of slatterns rushes in to wrap the tiny greasy-white body, now yelling at the top of its lungs, in a shawl, put it in a frayed little basket, and hang it from the ceiling.

Curse the vermin, but come come, little girl, may sweet Jesus protect you! And may your father use all his talents today, in the sunny square, to collect some decent alms!

Well, why not? These Neapolitan beggars are not small fry by any means, and Faustina's father least of all. How amusing it is to see him stand on the steps of the Duomo in the miserable uniform of his trade! Sometimes he trembles all over his body as he moans for bread, at other times he barely condescends to stick his nose over the snuffbox a passing cardinal holds out to him. On glory days, when no one is able to withstand his relentless pleading, he comes home mildly drunk and takes his firstborn, on whom he dotes, in his arms.

Faustina is a muscular little girl with big pink hands and shadows under her eyes. Until the age of ten her childhood follows the familiar pattern of stench, heat, dirt and the gorgeous sunlight that is absorbed at sunset in stripes of gold by the water of the bay of Mergellina. Then something changes, such a shame, but that's the way of things. Her mother succumbs to cholera and one bad day her father is knifed during a quarrel over a trivial matter of honour which arose when the beggar, who was stone-cold sober at the time, innocently asked a passer-by: what are you staring at, and the man had the gall to reply: at your stupid face.

It's just as well that the people of Naples are so devoted to charitable works. It is virtually impossible for a vagrant to starve in this city, and orphans are housed in an institution where they are raised with a view to employment in a rich man's house. By the time thirteen-year-old Faustina is delivered at the door of a *palazzo* with covered balconies, she is practised in a variety of skills ranging from slaughtering animals to stoking ovens for bread-baking, and anything else you can think of in between. In the grand house, where the kitchen is filled with as much busy chatter as the private quarters, people demand to know her name.

'Faustina Maria Della Papozze . . .'

Soon after this the young girl, on her knees and holding a soft woollen cloth, enters the world for which she is destined.

*

The Virtuoso

A maidservant is accustomed to silver and crystal. Her knees are familiar with the density of marble, wood, knotted wool, and her fingers know that brocade, a gleaming fabric bound with satin, must be carefully spread out after washing before it is allowed to dry outside, under the porch, in the fresh morning air. From the very first day Faustina feels a wonderful lightness in her breast, and she cannot understand from where it comes.

'Go on, sit down and have something to eat,' the cook has to remind the strong young lass after an entire morning spent in the storage cellar pressing the moisture out of a pile of cheeses. Faustina does as she is told and bends over a plate of soup, thinking drowsily of the heavy, hot flat-irons in the laundry room and still unaware of the true extent of her happiness. The realization doesn't come until one Friday afternoon when she's working herself into a sweat polishing the floor of the first-floor drawing-room and Paolo Caetani, the seventeen-year-old son of the master of the house to whom she will be devoted for the rest of her days, comes in to play a sonata before supper.

He sits down at the cembalo, preludes for a bit, adjusts his chair, plucks at his nose – he's a good-looking young man with a lock of powdered hair on his forehead – plays a piece with two sharps, looks up and sees the kneeling servant girl, propped on her short arms, staring up at him.

'And now for a song!' he says without a moment's hesitation.

Faustina is Neapolitan. She gets up from the floor and, barefoot, launches into a barcarole. The idyll has begun. The seventeen-year-old scion of an ancient family plays the accompaniment for the hoarse voice of a creature who exudes ardour and passion from every pore and knows very well that it would be wiser to transmute all that intensity into pure physical labour. And for five years, from 1694 to 1699, she does just that. Then one night, after having polished the delicate golden earrings belonging to Paolo's fiancée, she runs off with a snake charmer.

His name is Tristano Vico. Not only is he a beetle-browed charmer of snakes, he is also a wizard in red pantaloons as well as a quack doctor: standing on a dais in the marketplace, he stamps his heels and jabbers non-stop worse than a Capuchin monk, loudly extolling his brews, hey hey hey, illustrious ladies and fatuous gents, don't insult the good God with your boils ...! Faustina stands among the crowd of onlookers. She sees an individual prancing about in a devilish cadence and holding up a mirror in whose depths he can distinguish, as everyone knows, a frenzied spider: it is he who will sleep like a child in the crook of her naked shoulder tonight.

Who can determine the time and the place of a dream? One summer morning Faustina, fatter and older, stands waiting by the side of the road to Naples. She waves down a heavily laden wagon. She climbs into the back, then raises her hand to her forehead and narrows her eyes. All around her is sunlight. It is as if the inns, the starry nights, the black boxes with vipers, the curled golden eyelashes of her babies, twin boys who were born far too soon and far too soundlessly, and then Vito's singsong voice asking her one morning months ago already how she fancies his new two-tone teeth, before vanishing for good – she settles herself down, blinking her eyes – it is as if everything and everyone is encapsulated in that one, familiar moment of awakening: where was I in God's name?

The wagon driver drops her off at the harbour.

'Do you happen to know where Paolo Caetani lives?' she asks the first person she encounters.

He's not there. Faustina stands in the middle of a kitchen, her gaze fixed on a little girl with fiery red curls, holding out a white, loudly purring kitten to her.

'So Paolo . . .'

No no, he's away they explain all over again. The master, like so many of our barons, has departed on a big grey horse to Spain, to fight for Philip.

Giving in to the coolness and the scent of linden blossom all around, Faustina sits down at the table. She lays her big hands next to a big pile of broad beans. What is the name of this dear little girl?

'Angelica Margherita . . .'

Angelica Margherita, a cheerful three-year-old who has never known her mother and now lacks a father too, comes closer and clambers on to a chair, and there they are, the two of them, beans and kitten and all, presenting a most pleasing spectacle, and a year later they happen to be sitting there again when through the open door Faustina hears a footfall that she knows by heart. She looks up. In a pool of green-dappled sunlight stands Paulo. A man of some thirty years has come home, smelling of grass and animals.

What consternation, what a reunion of father and daughter and what jubilation when everyone in the house has come running! Then he sets eyes on Faustina. Clasping her elbows he draws her up and turns her around to face the light.

'You've grown a little moustache,' he says fondly.

A purple blush has risen in her cheeks.

Shortly after this the period of exile begins. The Habsburg on the throne of Naples deals out punishment. Punishment, eh? The villa lies at the foot of Vesuvius. The move from the city has been undertaken with snorting horses and gleaming wagons. Under the dark-blue sky the nights radiate love and everywhere lingers the smell of blossom and ash. Faustina lies in a wide bed under the eaves and although she is reconciled to whatever the happiness gathering in her breast has in store for her, the question is: whose love is it that is turning the whole region topsy-turvy?

The Virtuoso

Paolo has remarried and the following year, by the time Gisella has conceived, Faustina has moved into a pretty side-room with shutters, for she has become the confidante of the young bride, it is she who rubs the back and massages the small feet of the wife who, with all the nuances of an unbridled lust for life, never tires of dancing and playing, and whose sweet nature makes her the dearest of mistresses.

The infant is baptized Carlotta. The feasting continues.

This is life! This is breathing from early morning, when she lifts the kettle from the hob, till evening when dusk lures Faustina to sit out on the porch in the twilight with the baby on her knee and a white cat against her ankle, and to while away the hours without the least apprehension: all those oak saplings, all the cries in the distance and the barking, and the fortunate Paolo galloping up the drive on his favourite horse!

As if it were nothing special.

'But it is, it is,' Gisella tells her maid only a few years later. 'The organ's playing in the village. I can hear it, the *Divina Pietà* ...' It is August. The wind is becoming more parched by the day. A vein stands out under Gisella's heavy black hair. 'Come over to the window! Phew ...! Now the church bells are joining in too ...'

Faustina goes to the bedroom window and listens to the deathly silence of the afternoon until she hears a small sigh behind her back. God Almighty! My lady has collapsed! Faustina screams for help and rushes to and fro like someone demented and when Paolo, Angelica Margherita and even the toddler Carlotta and everyone else come running she beats her head with her fists, tears her hair and drowns in tears: what did she do wrong, the sweet thing lying in a heap on the floor, the gentle short-sighted eyes still staring in surprise?

A cold winter follows. A dry summer. The sap rises in spring all right, only to die down again when autumn comes. In Croce del Carmine, both in the big house and in the village, all things, slavish and torpid, have resolved to submit to Don Paolo, the man who has lost his true home. Paolo lives in a region where people have empty buckets and bowls standing around in grey courtyards of unrendered cottages, and where they look up from time to time from weeding a bed of turnips or cabbages to watch a swarm of black bees fly away over a steep hillside path. Faustina serves him, him and two lovable growing girls, you can't really say she's unhappy.

Could it be that this woman is too sere for the bittersweet seed of regret?

Nonsense, Faustina Maria Delle Papozze makes porridge. She irons ribbons. She who ushers Angelica Margherita's tutors into the study room every day – for this young girl is old enough for lessons in dancing and poetry – has the good sense to alert Paolo whenever any musicians turn up in the village. Greetings, my friends! she thinks, as she observes the inconsolable widower sweating and laughing as he drops into an armchair to get his breath back after a cadenza. She has noticed that each visit from such a company of fiddlers and pluckers, or, better still, a band of singers, is likely to set off a merry-go-round of faces and wigs and bonfires and, almost as in the old days, of strings of carriages drawing up at the villa which is still the home of two young heiresses.

Well, Angelica Margherita runs away and young Carlotta will notice with the passing of time that her marriage prospects are dwindling at her father's gaming table.

'Faustina, I've had a proposal!' Carlotta nevertheless announces when she has turned fifteen. And Faustina is sent to accompany the young bride to a country estate at Altavilla where she will comb hair and, in due course, take charge of two successive newborn infants.

One afternoon in March Faustina looks out of the attic window and sees a carriage and a wagon piled high with luggage approaching the house. She hurries downstairs just in time to see the love of her life, an invalid nearing sixty, step down from the vehicle. As she takes his hat he breaks into a smile, looking directly at her. What? Her heart skips a beat. Instinctively she takes a step forward, for in that one second she has seen that the hour of his dying has been fixed, this time he has not come temporarily, this time it is for good. Then she takes his arm. Knowing that her servants' hands will at last, now that this man's time is running out, perform their rightful task, she touches him with familiarity for the first time in her life.

'Fine . . . very good, thank you,' mumbles Paolo. 'Yes, by all means give me a hand.' And he says it in such a way that no one would dream of disturbing the couple as they shuffle up the stone steps. The vestibule is dark. The twosome pause to catch their breath. Faustina, incomprehensibly consoled, smiles.

Exiles, that's what we are, she thinks.

*

'Carry on as you please,' she tells a dainty white blouse. 'Off with you!' she commands the lid of a saucepan. 'Ah, you won't get away with that, you know!' A broom. Since her beloved has died, Faustina has taken to addressing objects. Why? Why . . . why . . . The essence of the riddle is, in the end, a question. Full stop. That's what she does, and what does it matter, besides: she is in good spirits, for where is she to spend the coming winter? Carlotta had barely buried her father before the dresses were ordered; Berto, Duke of Rocca d'Evandro, has promised his wife the immeasurable distraction of an opera season in Naples, for reasons only God and incidentally Faustina know. The old servant must accompany her. The first thing to strike Faustina in the city after all those years is the beggars.

And they speak every language in the world to boot!

For the rest everything revolves around beguilement, she recognizes that of course. Intoxication, dizzy spells – the whole city is in love and just look at Carlotta, look at Berto – are brought on as much by the volcano as by the sea and the squalid hovels, but it is the opera house above all else that leads the inmost soul into temptation.

'Faustina . . . I . . . it's that boy from our village, you remember, that angel . . .' stammers a feverish Carlotta, young, black-haired still, and thereby the image of her father and mother.

Faustina understands. Solicitous, she prepares a bath, she sprinkles powder; the mistress, who can hardly bear to remain in her husband's *palazzo*, wishes to be buttoned into a red bodice by her maid before she runs out into the street, because her heart is almost dying for love of a singer. Just so, a soprano. Just so, love. And that love is so ardent that when Gasparo, the *musico* in question, has to spend a month away in Genoa to sing on stage the presence of a French gentleman is required to assist Carlotta to continue breathing.

'Thank you kindly, madame,' says Rodolphe, Marquis of Sceaux, Count of Maillebois, to the wizened old woman who opens the door to let him in. Then he bows charmingly. Faustina quite likes the young man. She quite likes him and indeed feels sorry for him when he virtually disappears from the scene in December because

Gasparo is back in Naples singing Pergolesi, and the entire San Carlo, filled to the gods, is deflected from its course by the compass of that driving voice. Oh! What a handsome man! Not only Carlotta, impassioned in her box, cannot help sighing time and again, also Faustina is wholeheartedly present. Perched on a wooden bench in the pit, she thinks most of the singers are excellent. But there is only one Gasparo, so tall, so beautiful, in whose *aria amorosa* she detects such unabashed longing that she, elated in her black dress, thinks to herself: yes, of course, love, I know all about that . . .

Then suddenly the season is over. The weather is turning warm in Naples. On the morning of the twentieth of April a string of three carriages leaves the city through the Porta Capuana. Faustina knows why Carlotta, sitting next to Berto facing her, ignores the city disappearing behind them. Carlotta has already said goodbye, she did so a week ago by taking off with Gasparo to Rome on the spur of the moment; only yesterday did she return, dog-tired. The road climbs. The sky is empty. They make a halt at Santa Barbara to drink wine. Then come the meadows and the heat. Faustina chuckles at the sight of Carlotta resting her sleepy head on her husband's shoulder. First a novena to St Clare, she muses. Then I'll burn a Friulian viper and catch the smoke in her sheet. May I have chilblains if she isn't pregnant by St Peter-and-St Paul.

One Sunday in March the child is born. 'A son, if

you please,' Carlotta tells her delighted husband, 'made in Campano.' And then, by way of reassurance, she smiles sweetly at her two daughters, the elder of whom is already thirteen. A month later she asks Faustina: 'Did you hear the nightingale early this morning?' The two women are standing by a clothes-line in a field of flowers near the house. Faustina turns her head away. No, she heard nothing. But suddenly she feels a shadow falling across her face and because she is old and has been through so much, her thoughts wander. Nightingales? Surely they only sing at dusk? Looking up she notices for the first time the smile that Carlotta will from now on permit herself, mostly when the light is low, it's more like a glow, there's hardly any sadness, just a response to a fleeting salute from afar.

What's miserable? Having a headache and not looking at the trees. Lying awake and not sniffing and drinking.

This country house with its gardens and terraces is a far better place to spend the summer than the city! So anyone who wishes to come is welcome, but is kindly requested to disport themselves and to play with the children. Angelica Margherita, Carlotta and the Marquis of Sceaux – indeed, Rodolphe of the alert green eyes – decide to stage one of Sarri's chamber operas. Carlotta is given the lead role of servant-girl, much to the amusement of her husband, who is to play the continuo. Faustina! Faustina is instructed to dress her mistress, yes of course, at once, bonnet and shawl, the maids at

Rocca d'Evandro wear the latest fashion: waisted aprons with the prettiest scalloped hems.

Faustina kneels on the floor. She is embarrassed.

'Do you wish anything else?'

Yes, thank God. Since the duchess is rather fond of a pair of green eyes and quivers a little at the prospect of the coming, amber night . . . she would after all like to wear her rubies, her pearls and her gold bracelets.

Ah, how delightful! Just look at the servant-girl who is capable of producing the loveliest trills and turns!

But that's all gone. Gone is the summer and gone the years, the sun draws its golden arcs with mild persistence and each one may be the last. Berto is killed in a riding accident and Carlotta, his intimate friend, is devastated, and remains so. In mid-winter she sits by an open window. What can she be thinking of? The sky lies under a blanket of grey interrupted only in the distance, beyond the volcano where the sea laps the coast, by a sun-filled rift in the clouds. This thirty-five-year-old woman is so absent-minded nowadays that she doesn't notice that her old servant's strengths are failing fast.

What a to-do! Faustina gets everything mixed up: she thinks Carlotta's nostalgia is the same as Paolo's and she confuses his yearning with the deprivation that the dear God has seen fit to assign to her, Faustina's, life. She has stopped washing herself. In the kitchen she steps only on the red tiles. In the evenings when darkness falls she lights the lamp on the bedside table and then sits for hours staring with an expression of wonderment at the two large, chapped hands which she twists round and round.

Today she awoke with a dazzling idea. That's it: she will harness Cicotto! Upon entering the stable, it seems to her that the dear horse has been thinking along the same lines. In a while he will draw the two-wheeled chaise over the road, showing not surprise but rather relief, while she, just for the sake of appearances, holds the reins. Past the village, where the track curves and the acacias hang down over a rocky outcrop, Cicotto keeps up a gentle trot. Faustina beams. We're off! The sun climbs in the sky.

Afternoon heat. They rest by a watermill.

Evening. Cicotto grazes.

Night. Starry sky.

At daybreak Faustina still recognizes the distant hills, pale as a mirage, and she cries Giddy-up! Later that day, with the road shimmering ahead and a fat beetle flying alongside, buzzing so loudly as to drown the rattle of the wheels, she gives in to her drowsiness and leans her head against the wooden frame of the hood. Giddy-up, little creature, she plucks at her skirt, tomorrow we'll arrive, in this heat, in this melting light that sets the landscape ablaze as far as the eye can see with colours that a normal human being, in this life, cannot even dream of! It is May the eighteenth, 1747. Faustina Maria Delle Papozze strains with each of her five senses towards a fading void. Then her arm drops.

It is over.

VI

Is the lifespan of a man longer than that of a butterfly?

It is February now. I am riding across Naples in an open calash, in my coat pocket a letter from home. The sun is already pleasantly warm. My little daughters are eating and sleeping perfectly well. To deny that the arrival of the letter this morning merely inspired in me the desire to slip on my snakeskin shoes and run out of the house would be to lie. February. The season is just midway. It was only yesterday that the new programmes of the San Carlo and Fiorentini were announced in the *Gazzetta*. A church. A porch. Two women singers with a mongrel. Another church. The pungent odour of a fishmonger: they're frying fish in the open air. Everything looms and fades. I look around, full of memories and desires. By midday the ephemeral butterfly has already matured through countless experiences, yet it still has half a life before it.

So why think of farewell all of a sudden?

Why, on the via Giacomo, catch your breath all of a sudden at the sight of the February sun quietly yet with maddening intensity gaining ground from the winter?

I lean forward and poke the driver in the ribs.

'I'll get out here.'

When the driver takes my hand to help me down, he gives me a good-natured smile.

'Right, Maurizio . . . oops, I'm trembling all over!'

Gasparo's house is a few streets away. Hardly have I entered the hall, hardly have I started to unbutton my coat, than I stop and stare at the footman who let me in.

What's this I hear?

Way up above I hear singing, an unfamiliar voice. A sound, fresher than Gasparo's but also considerably less subtle, swooping in this house like a swallow, a harbinger of spring: I don't understand.

'A pupil,' the footman explains, taking my coat.

The moment I enter the music room the voice falls silent. I see a pale young man, his cheeks dusted with freckles, standing beside the cembalo, taking deep breaths. The impetuosity of the aria is still written all over his face. Then, suddenly humble, his eyes search out Gasparo's, which I know so well that I can tell as soon as something has touched the sunny side of his being. Gasparo lifts his hands from the keys. He jumps to his feet.

'Is there anything more sublime than such a string of

pure goat trills?' he cries, noticing me standing in the doorway.

Soon after it is he who is doing the singing, by way of example, and I watch, reclining on a divan flanked by potted palms and oleanders, trying to ascertain what the secret of this situation is. I am in an exalted mood. This morning, I was struck by the banal thought that everything is transitory.

'Listen here,' Gasparo addresses his pupil, completely relaxed after a terrible *passaggio* full of turns, 'what I mean is that you must expel the breath little by little, but still very loosely. Breathing is the most natural function there is. You're making too much effort.'

Words. Gasparo's speaking voice when he is explaining something about his most intimate world. There is no one who can explain who he is in words.

That winter he was my lover.

'From the beginning.'

The boy obeys. He expands his rib-cage, opens his mouth and lets me hear once more what I heard before.

Promising.

This Giuseppe, whose début in Rome has been fixed for April, is to become a familiar figure on the staircase of this house. He has travelled here from Venice with a letter of recommendation from Vivaldi, a priest who's a demon of a composer. Gasparo has conceded, half in good grace and half in irritation. All right then. For a month he will rule and watch over this young alto, who unfortunately has attempted to strengthen his muscles by piling bricks on his chest.

'. . . less pressure, my boy. A tiny breeze will do it.'

Lying full length, my cheek on my fist, I watch Gasparo, a grave expression on his face, pouting his lips and placing both hands on his pupil's flanks. He proceeds to give a commanding lecture on minimum expenditure of energy for maximum gain . . .

He gestures dismissively. 'Child's play, really.'

The light of February. On the open lid of the cembalo gleams a landscape in blue-green. I can smell the plants next to the divan, one of which, an oleander, holds its spiky leaves like a fan in front of my eyes. Two singers. Sometimes Gasparo sings, sometimes the angelic Giuseppino. Time and again the alto is interrupted by the soprano. Are the voices aware of a third participant at this lesson?

The duet being performed in this room is in reality a trio. When you keep the keys of a harpsichord depressed and someone sings the true notes, the strings will vibrate in sympathy. Nothing special about that, just the laws of acoustics. After months of exposure to Gasparo's discourses, little more is needed to make my sense of hearing, and other senses, vibrate in a wondrous manner.

'. . . Don't force things. The mechanism with which

you have been breathing since birth is the same as the one with which you sing . . .'

Our love affair is known all over the city. Naples is envious, but smiles and invites me nevertheless. At the glistening tables one can never gather too many admirers, who are always extra beautiful. Gasparo, of course, remains a god strayed from Olympus, but Carlotta's face, with such dark circles under her eyes, speaks volumes about the mystics of love. There is a universal voice exhorting all living creatures to unite. Carlotta is the worst affected. I protest, throw up my hands. Me, the worst affected? All right then, it's true. Gasparo lives in the theatre. Indeed, the erotic effect of a warm, draughty auditorium packed with people fixing their attention on you alone must be pretty overwhelming. But what else can start the whole matter? There are birds that only copulate when it rains. There are newly hatched snakes, with still tiny testicles, that are driven mad with desire at the first rays of sunlight. That my ardour is convincing is getting more obvious by the day. Let's go home, he says at a reception. Let's go upstairs and shut the door, take the wine with us, stoke up the fire . . . Tell me what to do.

'. . . Distribute your breath evenly. Don't push it. The muscles and the membranes in the throat need freedom.'

Come and lie closely with me, I say. Snuggle up to my back. Slip your right arm under my neck, hand on my breast, your left between my thighs, hand on my groin. All right? I ask. Surely it's all right? Fold your knees into mine. Now that you're lying with your exceptionally developed rib-cage pressed against my back I can feel exactly how you breathe. This bed is pleasantly, no gorgeously, soft. That I can feel the slightest movement of your ribs, Gasparo – and I'll take over that movement if you don't mind – is deeply reassuring in all sorts of ways. Time begins to percolate towards the four corners of the room.

'. . . loudness, volume, as if there is no end to it.'

But enough. I am entering the state of somnambulance already and eternity is an amusing notion, but my heart knows that some seasons will never revert to the cycle. Lie on top of me. Of all the people you know you want to make love to me most of all. It amuses you to fondle the zone above my garters like the next man. And I am not shy, not mistrustful, nor am I stupid. I nuzzle, nip, suck, prop myself up on my fists, raise my hips, twist my feet, lay my legs over your shoulders. Like a puppy joyously discovering a half-forgotten, carefully buried bone, I pounce on you. This is the moral and lyrical side of my nature. Never do I ask myself what your secret thoughts about me might be. Mildly puzzled, your eyes follow me to the window, where I rest my elbows on the sill, supposedly to observe the beautiful sky above the roofs of the city, a sky redder even than the sky in our village when the sun sinks behind the volcano and the fog rises so thickly in the fields that it is hard to even imagine the big, heavy bunches of grapes hanging between the leaves. Will you come? I ask over my shoulder. I have often thought that lovers, when making love, remain true to themselves. Nervous wrecks remain nervous wrecks, and half-wits remain half-wits. A confidence trickster in a black suit once left a few strange marks on my warm skin. A one-off like you remains a one-off. But the small sacrifice in your boyhood, which undeniably gave your talent more space, has not placed you outside the species. Sex is the core of the fundamental question of life. You are mysterious, soft, hairless, but by no means sexless, so take me in your arms. And aren't you growing more and more fond of me? Sometimes it's as if your attachment is that of a child. I'll do anything you want, anything, you say, you have only to ask. Your face becomes empty, a drowsy mystery, and I know what you mean: spin me a cocoon of guidelines. All right then, I say, let's breathe in and out like two lustfully intertwined godheads in an exotic land. You'll see, before you know it I will elicit from you, right from your own heart, unmistakably masculine desires. Now I bite, I mean kiss, you. Now I eat you, I mean devour, you before I lose my mind. But I take my time. Wouldn't you think it nice to prolong this wonderful state of affairs for a bit?

A gesture, a voice.

'Giuseppe . . .'

The young man, with an air of innocence but also some complacence, looks up from the sheet of music between his fingers.

'Now try doing the same thing with the tranquillo.'

At the sound of the first trills Gasparo takes a few steps to the window and stands with his back to the light. I can't make out his expression because of the glare, but I can feel the intensity with which he, motionless, arms crossed, traces the course of notes from lungs to sinus.

'Good,' he says after a brief silence. 'You're getting there.' His voice is lower than usual.

Then I hear the familiar drone again.

'Dramatic effects, coloratura variations, long cadences, now look here, everyone knows that sort of thing requires a surplus of air. But the point is, where do you get it from? No need to remind you that nature has blessed our type of singers with big lungs, and just as well, too. But I'll be frank with you, if you want us to remain friends just don't mention bricks, because the muscles you use for respiration . . .'

He breaks off. A look of anger crosses his face.

*

I can hear it too. Disaster is approaching. The moment I turn my head the door flies open and three men burst into the music room. They march up to Gasparo with bouncing tread. They have the faces of gangsters, but to my surprise they are wearing canary-yellow liveries of the latest cut. Muffled cries can be heard on the stairs as they bear down on Gasparo. This is serious. A raid. They grab hold of him. 'You're mad,' I whisper and rush forward.

'Come along,' one of the villains growls, 'you're coming with us!'

'Idiot, stupid ass!' snarl his two companions.

Gasparo, spluttering with rage, wrenches one arm free and lashes out. The huge fellow clutches at his midriff. At this his companions start grinning wickedly, Gasparo receives a blow under his eye. This is not the calmest of spectacles. I sink my nails into two evenly red cheeks.

A scuffle, and the shrill high voice of the singer. Then we are all propelled towards the staircase and Gasparo, locked between his captors, has to move his feet as quickly as he can to avoid falling flat on his face.

Out in the street a small crowd gathers. Passers-by swarm around the carriage emblazoned with the d'Elbeuf coat of arms, and watch as their favourite singer, gasping for breath, lurches into view.

'This fine gentleman is coming with us,' the lackey says, twisting Gasparo's arm behind his back.

Forgotten is the spring sunshine, forgotten the talented Giuseppe, the four-in-hand sets off at a furious pace. Shoulder to shoulder with Gasparo I bite my lips as I watch the last houses of the via Toledo disappear. Facing us sit two of the toughs. They didn't try to stop me when I squeezed myself into the coach as well, but at the first crack of the whip they brushed off their jackets and looked smug.

The Palazzo Reale, the harbour, and then a left turn. As we drive past the vacant lots along the road to Portici, I can feel Gasparo shaking. 'Hilarious . . .' I hear. I look sideways. My beloved, his shoulders hunched, is laughing so hard as to bring tears to his heavy-lidded eyes.

'Hilarious . . .' he repeats and turns to face me. One of his cheekbones is stained with a tender, purplish-blue bruise. 'D'Elbeuf?! Well well. The son-of-a-bitch!' He proceeds to explain the details of this matter of honour. D'Elbeuf, prince, duke, an admirer, indeed a generous one, has taken it into his head to precede his daughter's admission into the Convent of the Servants of the Eternal Adoration with a splendid feast at his country estate. Gasparo Conti, *musico*, star performer of the Royal Band of Musicians and so on and so forth, had put aside the letter imploring him to sing, he could not for the life of him think why, the fee was nothing short of eight hundred *zecchini*.

He chuckles again.

'The party would have been ruined . . .'

We travel at great speed. This is more like hovering than riding. From Naples to Portici the road is paved all the way. The mountains tremble from the blast of an explosion, birds fly up from the fields. Turkish slaves, their hair tied back in shiny ponytails, break the volcanic rock into small cubes.

Gasparo crosses his legs and tells me it's not always like this. On account of the markedly informational tone of his voice I say: 'Oh? not always like this?'

He nods. 'With less violence, but with a lot more scandal.'

Tell me.

It was in France, last year. The Lyons opera house was planning to stage *La Clemenza di Tito* with a celebrated Neapolitan in the leading role.

Gasparo glances away from me in the direction of the two gangsters, who respond by politely straightening their backs. 'For in that country they don't have a single good singer, but they do have masses of brayers. Anyway, I arrived in the middle of June. Do me a favour, I told the impresario, find me lodging in a house with a good view, and pay me an advance.' The gangsters nod understandingly.

To be sure, there was no faulting Beauregard. The castle, with slate saddle roofs and walls covered in white-blooming creepers, overlooked the same great river up which Gasparo had sailed that very afternoon on a ship from Marseilles. Upon entering the great granite-flagged hall at his host's side he could smell flowers and coffee and hear the silvery arpeggios of a harpsichord on which someone was playing, unmistakably, a piece by

Couperin. That same evening there was a grand reception. Lackeys flitted from table to table with champagne, there was dancing in the ballroom. Awed by the good looks of the foreign gentleman and shuddering at the reprehensible, criminal act that had been committed against his nature, the local dignitaries simply could not wait to hear him sing. 'Are you sure you're not too tired to sing us just one little song?' they wheedled. At midnight Gasparo mounted a semicircular stage and sang 'Nightingale in Love'.

'They're an odd bunch,' he says. 'During the day they're scared of white cats and at night of black ones, and they burn fires to keep the creatures away. They are just as fond of conversation as we are in Naples, but they talk about different things. There are two subjects they never tire of – warfare and the laws of nature – and they discuss them with equal ardour and in equal measure. Did you know they are convinced that, deep down in your heart, there's all manner of proper and moral inclinations?'

'Ah well, it's all the same to me,' I say. 'But how did they like the nightingale? What was it like for them to listen to the surpassingly perfect song of that little bird?'

The echo of his final tremolo. Tinkling glasses. Gasparo himself was surprised at his voice being so well disposed in spite of his journey, and it was some time before he noticed that following each brief burst of applause the guests whispered awkwardly among themselves, that is if they weren't giving him condescending looks. Later, during supper, he was given what was supposed to be a seat of honour next to a toothless heroine aged at least seventy, and was expected to reply to questions he was unaccustomed to. All this should, of course, have warned him of what was to befall him in the theatre later that week.

'I don't know if you've ever had any dealings with them?' he inquires just as we are all thoroughly shaken about because one of the horses has stumbled.

'Yes, I have,' I say. 'They have hazel eyes, curly eyelashes, dark hair on their lower arms and they prefer a shorter cut to their jackets than the men here. As for love, they show a keen interest in it, almost as much as in optical experiments. Impressed as they are by mathematics, they believe that each historical truth is no more than a likelihood.'

Calmly I look past him. Two of the king's galleys glide across the smooth surface of the bay. Twice twenty-two men dipping twice twenty-two oars into the water, in perfect unison. The volcano is hazy. The grey-white plume of smoke curves to the right, from where I'm sitting.

'And besides,' I say, 'I never met one who didn't lug the complete works of Molière around with him in his suitcase wherever he went.'

No entrance on horseback. No golden boots. No page with a giant fan made of feathers. Upon being told at the first rehearsal that one of his arias had been scrapped, so that he would have to spend the entire second act standing behind the *prima donna* with nothing to do, Gasparo turned on his heel and left without a word. The differences were resolved. The *maître*, nervous and forty-ish in a brown velvet waistcoat, had paid him a visit after lunch in Beauregard and had apologized so profusely that the next morning Gasparo, notwithstanding the insult he had suffered, had produced the most wonderful sounds for the orchestra and his colleagues to hear. Everything seemed to be all right, but there was another incident during the afternoon of the première, when Gasparo suggested concluding the first act with *Son qual nave che agitata*.

'*Son qual nave che agitata*?' echoed the *maître* incredulously from behind the harpsichord.

'*Son qual nave che agitata*.'

'But that's about a shipwreck!'

Gasparo did not bother to reply, but stared with imponderable fascination at the skulls and wigs of the members of the orchestra in the pit, stood on the stage.

'That aria belongs in a completely different opera . . .'

The singer fished his watch out of his waistcoat pocket. 'Right you are.'

'. . . and so it's utter nonsense.'

Conductor and musicians bowed their heads together, whispering. Gasparo exercised patience. Then he said, not without irritation: 'Dotted leaps, glissandi of varying pitch and volume, trills in all sorts of lengths. Devil take it, why did I come all the way here?'

But there was no giving in and evening fell. And evening turned into night. That night in the red theatre, icy silences descended over the audience, or there was deliberate coughing, and many people left their seats and joked as they made for the foyer to have supper while Gasparo sang his soli. The truth was, in the eyes of the French public a male soprano was simply absurd.

'What! . . . What . . .?' I stammer. I cannot help turning my gaze on the two villains sitting opposite, and yes, to be sure, they're furious too. For a while we exchange looks of the deepest shared indignation. Do we really have to envisage Gasparo actually standing there and singing, alone as in death, on the edge of that precipice of cold incomprehension? Trills are confidential. Sixteenth passages: utter dedication. The faultless leap to a high B is purely a matter of trust. Virtuosity is innocence. I stare into a pair of flushed faces, one of which is scratched and rather ugly. Is it possible that such people exist, people in their right minds who turn their backs on a soprano merely to gossip about spirit and matter? Deeply hurt, Gasparo had sat on a stool in his dressing-room after the performance.

A sharp bend. Two rows of laurel bushes hurtle past and the thud of the hooves is drowned out by the crunch of gravel on a drive. We are reaching our destination. On a hillside we catch sight of a house flanked by mighty-crowned trees. The driver abruptly reins his horses to a halt at the foot of a marble stepped terrace. All four of us are thrown together, as we regain our composure we catch a glimpse of a plump azure-clad figure standing squarely in our path: d'Elbeuf, whose heart is set on hearing a certain singer today, come what may, because his daughter is entering a convent.

We step down from the carriage, Gasparo goes first. As soon as my feet touch the ground I sense an atmosphere of great sympathy. Dogs bound towards us, windows open and people lean out to wave and clap their hands with the happiest faces imaginable, and not without reason, for even before we reach the front door Gasparo has launched into a *Confitebor tibi*, a delightful psalm in B flat which, being composed in a tripartite da capo form, initially recalls all the joys of the operatic aria, but on this occasion, where a young girl dances about in dazzling finery before donning her nun's habit for good, it has the effect of a minuet in minor, of a dance melody that is oddly consoling in the whirl of a quasi-cheerful triple time. *Memoriam fecit* sings Gasparo at the top of his voice as we reach the garden room, and looks around eagerly for the daughter, who steps forward, tall and fair-haired, from a circle of friends into a garland of clear notes, an ornament that embellishes and qualifies the grave motif of F, B flat and G, not by way of counterpoint to this gravity, but by way of distortion, for on this day the girl, splendid in her youth and brocade, will as yet be embraced with the greatest tenderness by all.

Words have meaning, as do musical notes. What happens when the two colossal systems of language and music unite? I feel drunk the moment Gasparo begins to recite *Et in saecula saeculorum*, although I and all the other guests are hearing nothing new, we know the words by heart. And in the century of centuries: adrift, more fleeting than the most fleeting memory, the concept floats across the sun-filled room while the soprano harnesses the syllables in a rising chromatic line, drowsy, searching, leaving behind the adventure of B flat major and skimming along the highest notes of his register before entering a G minor phrase. Why is the light so beautiful and rosy? Why is even an old dog under a table with its head resting on its paws, motionless but for the watchful eyes, part of the idyll? In the crowd of strangers I discover several familiar faces. By a stained-glass window sits a scarlet Angelica Margherita. Next to a cupboard decorated with carved lions' heads stands my husband and also the Frenchman Rodolphe, a faint smile on his lips.

'I still think it's most peculiar,' the latter will confide in me minutes later. 'A male voice reaching such high notes. The timbre isn't natural either.'

And I will look at him and acknowledge his green-eyed glance with civility. Rodolphe, the twenty-five-year-old *marquis* who was sent on tour by his father, beamed as soon as he noticed me among the guests.

'I don't quite know, sir, what you mean by natural. All I know, as you do, is that the centuries go by and that everything either vanishes or is transformed. The pavane becomes a bourrée, the hero turns serving-girl, the Spanish veil a velvet ribbon around the throat. Besides, we all know that at some time in the future, be it in the early-morning hours or on a day full of sun and birdsong, each one of us will mumble a final word which will not necessarily be truthful or even remotely relevant.'

He laughs and grasps me by the shoulders.

'Carlotta . . . why . . .'

'Listen,' I say, still somewhat flustered. 'Did you hear how curiously he ended that psalm?'

Gasparo sings *amen* and ah, how strange I feel suddenly. His eyes flxed on a garland of silk flowers he has the cheek, capricious as he is, not to finish the song with a leap to a higher octave the way it is written, but to conclude the somersaults of the *saeculorum* with the heart-rending, beseeching interval of the seventh, whereby that eternal last word, that commonplace, that *amen*, suddenly sheds its conciliatory nature to take on a different meaning today, entirely in keeping with our melancholy mood: 'Oh?', 'But why must it be so?', 'Oh, is that really so?'

Cheering and relief. 'Serve the ices now,' says d'El-beuf's wife. When Gasparo in his tight-fitting white breeches inclines his handsome body to gather up some sheets of music from the cembalo, it is the familiar impassive cast of his features that makes me think: impossible ever to leave him!

Then the Frenchman turns up at my side. 'Come along, come outside for a bit, into the sunshine.'

In the garden the rose bushes are still bare.

'It cut through my heart like a knife,' I say.

*

Night is falling. It is dark and some of the guests feel the cold on the terrace overlooking the sea. You too, Carlotta, suffer goose-pimples for the sake of a look at the stars and the crescent moon. They look so brand-new and yet so timeless. That luminous glow, you hear the Frenchman explain painstakingly, is caused by myr-iads of stars invisible to the naked eye, he asks his host for a telescope. You are not surprised when the latter excuses himself. D'Elbeuf took you round his sculpture gallery this afternoon, he is not averse to gazing upwards, he explained, but prefers to look downwards. He showed you the gods, men and animals of marble which he has hauled up from a well beside a very ancient amphitheatre nearby. Carlotta, dear friend, do spare a moment to inspect the small terracottas.

See the clarity of the form? That sweeping curve?

A glass in your hand, you sense the nearness of the sea and of eternity. A nocturnal bird swoops past. Such birds are always hunters. They perceive the tremors of another animal and dive down from the sky. A cry and then silence once more. The musicians in the house have stopped playing, but the party is not yet over. A girl bedecked with diamonds wanders about like a sleepwalker, not one carriage has left yet. The drivers stand around in small groups, they drink wine and eat meat-filled pancakes. Later, when the time of departure comes, they will light torches.

Just a moment! Someone tugs at your sleeve. You turn and before you know it a note is pressed into your hand, a servant vanishes. Then, for the first time today, you feel truly serene.

Let's leave now, you read by the light of the candles in the hall.

After the tumult of the party, the soft darkness of the carriage. You finger the fine gold chain round his neck. Like eight men out of ten, Gasparo wears the scapular of the Virgin of Carmine. You'd had enough, hadn't you? you say, you wanted to get away. You bring your lips close to his warm face and you are not in the least ashamed to say: you're mine, I found you and now you're mine. Will you remember me for ever? You can hear him chuckle. He's had an enjoyable day and his fee was princely. Did you see the first violin? he asks. That stout little fellow who couldn't help laughing during his saltarella? He's promised me an interesting hour or two tomorrow to show off his new harpsichord. The instrument is of Prussian design and, just fancy: a keyboard, quite normal, and four or five stops that enable you to imitate the sounds of a guitar, a harp and, so it seems, even a viola d'amore. And you can also shift the keyboard to transpose any piece you like a half or whole tone lower, even a minor third.

Love is the art of captivation. The action requires talent, but a little forbearance can't do any harm. It's only February. A carriage draws up at a house on the via San Carlo. Shall I tell you how, by taking a very deep breath, not too deep of course, you can stay afloat among summits of passion so lofty that you think, in retrospect, this was simply not human? You have arrived. The front door opens. In the room facing west a small fire of scented logs casts a glow causing the red patterns on the walls to blur and sway like aquatic, somniferous blooms. Unhook my dress.

VII

I keep running into Giuseppe these days. He is lodged in the house on the via San Carlo. Often his face is so pale that all you notice are the wolfish yellow eyes. He overtakes me on the stairs with nimble steps. Why the hurry? I call out. When he looks round I see the fever, so familiar to me, of someone whose heart, head and senses are all tangled up. In a week or two he will be on stage. All he thinks of, it seems, is the afternoons when his voice grows more and more agile and free. Then I picture his tutor. The face with the rounded jaws. Gasparo keeps his gaze fixed on you and listens most attentively.

Personally I would find it unbearable.

So now I am looking for a friend to listen to my endless chatter in the afternoons. Because that is my solution: the stream of words that I must forgo is now to be produced by me. I spend the hours reserved for lessons strolling around the harbour with Rodolphe and telling him all I know about Gasparo.

It is a leaden day. Rodolphe and I follow the path between the ramparts of the Castel Nuovo and the low quayside. There are many people about, talking in small clusters and singing. It is not cold, the wind is moderate. Rodolphe listens to my story about how, a few years ago, Gasparo was persuaded by a stout composer from Saxony to sail for England and to perform there under the most favourable conditions.

'Because on that great island people will do anything, truly anything, to hear a singer!'

I can feel Rodolphe watching me out of the corner of his eye, and without looking at him I know what his expression must be. Affectionate and ironic.

'To start with,' I say, 'they offered him a retainer of eighteen hundred pounds.'

'Wonderful,' the voice said next to me. 'That's fifty thousand *sous*. Enough to feed all the poor in Paris for a week.'

I am amused by his voice, not misled. I know Rodolphe is listening to me for a purpose, he intends to draw me out so as to dissuade me from certain things that have nothing at all to do with the slums of Paris. What happens when you give his rational arguments just the teeniest nudge with the tip of your doeskin shoe? Emotion, upheaval, and jealousy against a background of an admittedly impressive four-poster bed in a room on the seafront, on the Chiaia, with a view of the clouds above the sea and a forward-tilted mirror at the foot of the bed.

How interesting it is to be both observer and participant! I am determined to steer this conversation, fascinating as it is, in the direction of my choosing.

Playing for time, I drawl: 'Naples spends fortunes on the opera, but the first beggar has yet to starve in the streets. Say, how about a stroll on the pier?'

Beyond the fortress lies a small square. If you want to return to the city you can do so by passing through two tall gates on your right hand. Rodolphe and I stand still. The giddiness that comes over me I attribute to the mighty bows of several galleons looming up suddenly in the harbour. The light is uncanny, there is a rain cloud in the sky. We turn left on to the pier, and walk all the way to the stone steps at the far end. Screaming gulls. A swift dinghy with four panting men. In a rush of elation and premature lovesickness I tell him the story: one day in October Gasparo scudded up the Thames to London on a hundred-and-twenty-ton vessel in full sail.

The weather was exceptionally fair. Little puffs of white cloud in the blue sky. Gasparo stood on the upper deck, directly under the mainsail, he could sense the proximity of the port. The smell of the water grew sweeter, the river busier. Stately sailing ships in full rigging shot past each other in opposite directions with only inches to spare, closer to the bank the river was swarming with small craft. Gasparo raised his arm and shaded his eyes with the flat of his hand. His shirt unbuttoned at the throat, the hair tied in the neck, the born singer surveyed the embankments with his theatre-trained eyes. Very good. He sniffed appreciatively. Beyond a foreground of small buildings, in the spire-studded distance, gleamed the huge dome of St Paul's Cathedral.

Gentle pressure on my arm. Rodolphe interrupts me.

'Carlotta!'

I take my time to react.

'What's the matter?'

'What's the matter?' He lays his hand on the nape of my neck and twists my head from side to side. 'There's a shower of rain ahead of us and a low sun behind, just look!'

I see the rainbow. It is formidable, its bands an uncommonly bright red, orange, yellow, green, blue – the surface of the bay is glassy, opaque, like the ships – dark blue, violet. Rodolphe, sensing my wonder, takes the opportunity to bury his nose in the hair behind my right temple.

I protest. 'Get along with you!'

But his breath is pleasantly warm as he speaks softly into my ear: '. . . it is caused by the sun's rays refracting in the drops of rain. Because the different colours refract at slightly different angles, we see the reflected rays so tidily arranged.'

Such order! We kiss among the stakes and ropes on the breakwater. The secret of light neatly decoded before my very eyes! Yet as I detach myself from his arms I take the liberty to think: so what! And I survey the iridescent adventure as meekly as before. Behind the first arc emerges a second, less distinct, one. The order of the colours is reversed. This time the outer band is a radiant violet, the inside red. In spite of what I have just learned my thoughts, incorrigible vagabonds, go their own way. The world I know is a beautiful but somewhat haphazard accumulation of facts. From time to time I acquire knowledge by means of systems that are certainly not the most simple. From one wonder I reach, in full command of my senses, to the next.

'In future . . .,' Rodolphe begins.

Can't he see that I have removed myself to a slightly higher plane? From where I'm standing it's not at all hard to see the radiant arc in the sea at Naples as a grandiose welcome to Gasparo, when he was received in London a few years ago.

The population of the Anglo-Saxon city was expecting him. The *Daily Journal* had published so many long and detailed reports of the singer's exploits that some people thought: what a load of rubbish. But mostly the fervour in the streets and taverns focused on the central issue.

Will this twenty-five-year-old Adonis surpass his rivals? Can he reach higher notes? Does he sing louder? Softer? With more artistry? Is his lung capacity greater? Red faces took on a glassy expression.

Want to bet?

Gasparo and Handel hit it off at once. The composer, having been in the service of the court for years, had been exposed to agonizing competition for the past few seasons, and felt he had at last found himself the right singer. One morning the two of them sat and talked in the empty Covent Garden theatre. Picture this. The portly, skull-capped figure of the 'dear Saxon' spreading out piles of music on his desk, the tall Neapolitan affably poring over the sheets. Not only the configurations of notes aroused his interest, it was also the composer's agitation. Without knowing quite what was going on, Gasparo's excursions into the city had left him keenly aware of a spirit of dispute. Statecraft or entertainment, what could all the fuss be about? He sensed that there was something afoot from which he, a singer, was by no means excluded.

Gasparo looked at the composer, huge, double-chinned, with the apparent strength of a buffalo. He agreed to sing not only in operas but also in church and at court.

Well now, the court. Gasparo had hardly entered the palace gate than he sensed anew the flow of unrest and discord. 'Here we are, Sire,' said Handel and introduced the singer to the king. Flanked by courtiers in splendid attire, King George II and his son sat on red velvet. Gasparo bowed. The king seemed to glow with contentment, but the Prince of Wales struck him as unaccountably ill-tempered. Gasparo sang a few Italian solo cantatas and then five English songs, all of them composed by Handel himself. The more appreciative the king was, the sulkier the prince became. When the father remarked that Gasparo's pronunciation of English made him sound like a Welshman, the son rose and stormed out from under the canopy.

'Don't mind him,' said Handel. 'They're always at loggerheads.'

That Saturday the two men performed in St Paul's. The spirit of friendship had taken possession of them. And the Londoners, ever eager for a fair contest, went in droves to witness the sensational encounter between two champions. Cacophony, silence. Vibration. In a cathedral overflowing with people Gasparo, accompanied by the opera musicians, sang the part of Mordechai. And he did so with such emotion, such dedication, that this biblical hero, whose part had to be played here without recourse to the smallest gesture because the Bishop of London had banned all acting in church, was as impressive as any Achilles or Hector. An awestruck congregation, and no rest in the intermission. It was Handel's turn. The master, in high spirits, poised his agile, stubby, pale hands over the organ keys and played a concerto specially composed for the occasion which, in spite of the genius of its polyphony, was so easy on the ear that even the pigeons in the furthest corners of the belfries were not unaffected by it.

Afterwards the public flocked to Covent Garden to buy tickets for the opera.

Gasparo sang there in the following months. He sang in Handel's *Lothario*, in *Poro* – the composer had not minded in the least when the virtuoso singer inserted a few arias of his own – and he sang in an opera by Hasse, the libretto in Italian but with recitatives in English adapted by Handel. Under the spell of success it did not occur to either Handel or Gasparo to talk about anything but sharps and flats – and money of course. But one day, when they were drinking port in the Crown and Anchor, Gasparo had looked around him in surprise.

'Why is everyone here so excited?' he asked his friend.

Then Gasparo heard that the city had two passions. The opera, for one. There was murderous competition from a rival company at Lincoln's Inn Fields. And then there was philosophy. Folly and insight, on that island, formed an exemplary couple. In the salty wind carrying the smell of fish and tar, people had, as far as life's problems were concerned, come up with some clever solutions. Everyone delighted in them. Knowledge and ethics? The subject remained as light as a dream during those interminable hours of discussion, for both the devil and God himself maintained their reassuring presence. God is the proof of our humanity. Common sense, on that side of the Channel, had a touch of glory before it blew across to France.

In a tavern full of soothsayers and dice players a somewhat tipsy composer poured out the last drops of wine. His inquiring eyes sought out those of the singer. 'Are you interested in Locke, Berkeley, Hume by any chance?'

*

'Ha ha,' mocks Rodolphe, 'Just the kind of subject to interest our friend, I'm sure!'

His interruption annoys me. I turn to face him but he grabs my hand and pulls me along. We race down the pier like idiots. The whole sky is flooded purple, the arc has gone. By the time we reach the city gates my face is wet from the rain.

The evening finds us all in the San Carlo again. The box in which I float is a little boat lined with velvet and mirrors. Which way will it go? In the distance stands Gasparo. He is singing one trill after another. I'm sitting in the audience. Are you far away or close by? I can't bear to think there is space in our intimate world for third parties.

Whenever there is no soprano aria to be heard we turn away to chat amongst ourselves. Rodolphe orders coffee and liqueur and wins me over by asking me things and listening to what I have to say. But if I'm not careful he'll start talking about art and music, and try to get me into a corner with shrewd arguments. Luckily Angelica Margherita is at my side today. My elder sister is just the person to squash all too rapid judgements. Sometimes all she does is arch an eyebrow, thin as a blade. I look admiringly at her imposing throat and breast, the softness and whiteness so subtly framed by a frock of red moiré silk.

'Well now, I'm getting quite carried away.'

That's just Rodolphe's cynicism, and we don't react. Our conversation about high art, which is not adversely affected by barbarism and bad taste – quite the opposite, in fact – has to wait until after an aria has been repeated twice on account of wild cheering from the audience. Gasparo in the role of classical hero, an exile who has been washed ashore on an island, wears a modern gala uniform and a plumed hat. Instead of going down on his knees before the tyrant, he gives a condescending little bow. Instead of allowing himself to be drenched in brine, he moves to the wings for a glass of water. He gestures impatiently to the musicians in the pit, can't you speed things up a bit?

Rodolphe thinks the story is being perverted. Could anyone ever take this clown for a hero in antiquity?

We, my sister and I, say: of course it's possible. He: you can't be serious, that ridiculous uniform I can forgive, and also the wig. But not his disdain for the banished prince, who once, long ago, had to swallow his pride to spare the life of his sister. You must admit that's a bit much. We say: art is a question of conjunction. Form attaches itself to content and then the proper work begins. Why don't you order some more drinks?

'Wine? Grappa?'

'Muscatel wine, *marquis*.'

'Shall we have something to eat too?'

'Yes please.'

Then Rodolphe says he knows perfectly well that a story, if it is to gain access to the soul, must be thoroughly shaken like a bush because the soul is irresistibly attracted by the aroma of other things, behind the true meaning of the words.

We watch him walk to the door of the foyer. He gestures to a lackey and returns. In the oval mirror we see his intelligent, candle-lit green eyes. Go on then, we say, tell us all about it. We agree with you. What sort of aroma might that be? Which tastes can you suggest? He pulls a rather serious face and says: in the first place God. We nod with approval. God, he continues, is the product of fear, of love, or simply of veneration, and as soon as you try to make out whether he's the beginning or the end, you come up against the question of the chicken or the egg. My sister and I are shocked into silence. And then, continues Rodolphe, there are the moral principles.

It goes without saying that we, being in search of the best within ourselves, can handle the most complicated intrigues about valour, honour and fidelity.

A young man in a high-collared jacket brings the wine. We draw our chairs close together. Your health! And yours! Violins and a voice can be heard vaguely in the distance. Very well spoken, we say, to start up our conversation again, the trouble is, though, that we find ethics without God a dreadful bore. In this country we have great respect for prophecies and propitiation, for the transmigration of the soul, for blind spots, for ingenuous and wondrous hypotheses and for notions that aren't always equally lucid. Rodolphe fumbles in his pockets for tobacco. He says: I suppose you could of course be interested in beauty alone. Indeed so, you lift up an arm, pat yourself on the head, drift off into nothingness and think, well well, what a splendid, delightful work of art! Just my taste!

We pause for a while to admire the stage-setting for the second act. The waves of a stormy sea roll jerkily from left to right, they are activated from underneath by a set of cables pulled by incredibly strong stage-hands. Ships are tossing on the waves. Twenty dancers perform their ballet in the same rhythm. Amid the sound of clanking metal and string music a few singers come on stage, one of them, a female soprano, steps forward with a little dog in her arms. We are so bold as to maintain, we tell our companion, that by translating the plot of a story into pure virtuosity, it becomes entirely intelligible. Why is this place sold out night after night? The fabulous scene unfolding on stage is not acted out, it is real. Highly cultivated craft attaches itself to an old notion about heroes. Control of the muscles of tongue and throat. A lyrical, heartfelt cry, emitted in one long *vocalise*, is vertiginously prolonged with a series of very rapid head notes. Do we have to explain that all this is about courage and deepest religious sentiment?

The woman sings very well. She lets go of the little dog. The creature sits high and dry among the waves, so to speak, furiously biting its coat. Enter Gasparo. Presently the solo will be followed by a duet. This is sheer provocation of plausibility, dear ladies, Rodolphe tells us, not to mention of good taste. My sister and I flap our fans up and down in front of our eyes. The spectacle in the distance flickers. Burnished gold, brass tones and a dimly remembered story about a royal prince and princess. Holy Virgin! God! we think, we will endure the dramas of our lives uncomplainingly! We say: my dear *marquis*, gentle Rodolphe, the plausibility content of this evening is very high. All of us here share real passion, real anger, real deceit, common impulsiveness and a forgiving nature. Do not bore art with good taste, sir. All that fancy talk... Simplicity, purity! says

Rodolphe, raising his voice. I foresee a future . . . All that fancy talk about life and art, we persist heartlessly, makes us fear the worst for both.

The female singer falls silent and gestures to Gasparo. Now it's his turn.

'Alas for art,' we mutter, 'Simplicity, purity, what isolation . . .'

My sister and I lean back. Our arms touch familiarly. But we are no longer four eyes which, cheerful and communicative, enjoy a private joke from time to time. From one moment to the next I am filled with melancholy. Twice already I have been reminded of the future . . . The cock will crow thrice. I twist my head this way and that, beseechingly, scanning the audience. My glance meets Giuseppe's. He is standing in the third box on my left, he recognizes me and smiles. I smile back at him with sudden fondness, for my melancholy immediately extends to *his* treble, too. Dear boy, do you realize that it's as if you don't belong anywhere? We look at each other. Pale eyebrows, the face mask-like, his inscrutable smile is enough to make anyone weep.

'Who's that?' asks Angelica Margherita.

I tell my sister – she wants to know if he and Gasparo have become lovers yet – I tell her I don't know, I simply cannot imagine their passion.

My sister raises her glass in a heartening toast: the umpteenth prediction. Then we both start thinking of the houses and *palazzi* waiting outside, under the dark sky. Why not leave the allusions of this ghostly hour for what they are?

A noisy crowd has gathered on the piazza Carolina. Fires are burning and we hear loud voices. Tomorrow is the Day of the Ships, the stalls are already being put up. My sister and I join the straggling crowd of drinkers under the awnings. The proprietress of a tavern splashes wine into pitchers which fleet-footed children deliver to customers. Further away a mock battle is being fought, in the light of torches we see four men brandishing knives, they don't flinch, but spit and bare their teeth. I like it here. I cling tightly to a clamorous, self-inhibiting present. A fortune-teller squats in front of us. We nod and hold out our hands. The old woman smells of vinegar, she sees a future of weddings, fountains, grass and flowers. It is not until she lifts up her face to us that we see her empty eye-sockets. Suddenly she lays her searching hand against my cheek. She says she is listening and can hear the wind whistling through bundles of twigs in winter.

I go home with my sister. I sleep in her arms.

*

Do you know how wonderful it is to be alive? I lay my arm around his waist. My glance comes to rest on his thick white eyelids, I can hear him snoring peacefully, presently I shall fire my questions at him. The questions in my head are reasonable, but they are random, I long above all to hear the somewhat reedy speaking voice I have been so painfully deprived of for days.

Tell me about England. Why were there two opposing parties? What was it all about?

It is two in the afternoon. Gasparo and I joined an excursion party to the island of Capri this morning. As we set sail we could feel the day was going to be hot. The wind was favourable. Restless as I had been for days, I could not make up my mind whether to stay with the other guests – there were about eight of them – or to wander off to the stern to be alone. Spray, creaking ropes and ten yards away white fish, as big as herrings, leaping up out of the waves. Sea-cats. An array of sky, water and shore danced before my eyes, then I saw Gasparo. He was sitting on a wooden bench, his shoulders hunched, and for once he was ignoring the admirers gathered around him. He wore the blankly grave expression deaf people sometimes wear.

How little we have talked lately!

At midday a meal was served on deck. Captain Luca Maria San Silvo, who had taken care to provide a table with oysters and a selection of wines from Capri, told us the names of all the sails. The ship gathered speed. From under the mizzen we saw the sun-soaked island come into view. We were greeted by a cannon salute. Soon after that some of the guests went ashore, others stayed on board for a siesta in the cabins.

What can be more peaceful than a ship moored in a still blue bay? I like dozing next to a sleeping man.

He opens his eyes.

'It was a feud for the sake of a feud,' he yawns. 'You know how it goes.'

Still half asleep he scratches his scalp.

'Suddenly everyone gets angry and remembers the oddest things. The singers deserted Handel, he grew fat and drank too much. His best singers were lured away by the Opera of the Nobility, a company of rich people who threw their money around . . .'

I listen with melting heart. 'Oh,' I cry. 'I cannot imagine them deserting him. What had he done to them?'

'His side lost Senesino, Montagnana, Bertolli . . .'

Gasparo counts off his fingers. I take his hand and lay it on my stomach.

'Yes?' I whisper urgently in his ear.

He raises his hand again and spreads four fingers.

'. . . and Gismondi.'

I give him a kiss. 'How awful,' I say softly.

He nods.

There had been a scandal. The king favoured Handel, his son sided with the enemy. One newspaper supported Covent Garden, the other backed Lincoln's Inn, and the same went for the public. Heated debates and impassioned pamphlets were devoted to the performances, to the singers and to Handel, who kept up the fight from his desk, consummate and dignified, dashing off one *Terpsichore* after the other *Oreste*. Then, just as people were beginning to lose track of what the dispute was really about, Gasparo had appeared on the scene.

'They were dying for me to come.' He turns his face towards me. I can feel his breath. 'Poems were delivered to my house day after day.'

He reminisces with visible satisfaction. I am utterly content. Secure in the knowledge of the love that awaits me, I'm perfectly happy to dwell for a moment on this: London, December, a very curious performance is being given in Covent Garden. Being pressed for time, Handel has contrived a *pasticcio*, an *Artaserse*, for which he has scraped together pieces written by himself, Hasse, Vinci and several others. This hardly promises to be a night of profound emotion, you would think. Yet from the first instant the house is filled with a fever more consuming than the seven-day swamp fever, and a desire more wrenching than heartbreak. Everyone is waiting for the Neapolitan soprano. There he is. Just in time, in other words: there is an excruciating moment's delay before he emerges in his heroic costume and steps forward.

The audience seethes.

'I couldn't tell you what exactly was going on,' says Gasparo, 'but by the time we were halfway, the *Despair ye not* during the second act, I noticed that the orchestra was playing increasingly thinly. At first the whole string section played with spirit and fine tone, and also the oboes and bassoons were excellent. Believe me, I have rarely performed with more able musicians, but as you can guess, there was something afoot. By the time I started my andante, the violas had fallen silent and the bassoons were playing too high. Now bassoons are always quick to go out of tune so that didn't surprise me too much, though I needn't tell you how very odd an orchestra sounds when the violas are missing. After about fifteen bars something happened with the continuo: while the harpsichord played on with great clarity and precision, it was as if the cellists were on the bridge of a ship in a tempest, because one moment you would hear a tone like a shot from a cannon, and the next nothing at all. No, you'd expect me to get quite confused by all those clever effects, but I didn't. Because you see, when all was quiet except for the harpsichord, which Handel himself was playing – the audience was extraordinarily quiet, too – I suddenly had this urge to find out how far you can go in *mezza voce*, singing very softly in a big, crowded space. Anyway, I was just beginning to feel like a lark in the sky when that idiot came tottering across the stage. Well, to call him an idiot is a bit unfair, I'll explain in a moment that he actually meant well, but I was telling you about *mezza voce*. It's quite straightforward, but not easy. You get everything, throat, mouth cavity, ready exactly as you would for the full voice, you even exaggerate a bit, and then you curb the force of the breath as if you were driving a team of Neapolitan thoroughbreds across the narrowest of . . .'

A stranger appeared on stage. He was a stocky, big-boned little man, and with the disconnected air of a somnambulist he had clambered up the six steps on the side of the platform. His lips trembling, he crossed from the golden pilaster marking the beginning of the scenery all the way to the far end of the stage, where Gasparo was singing his lilting *Alas, whither will fate take me?*.

It was John Christopher Swift, the first viola player. The musician had, a few moments ago, felt his heart lurch at the beauty of the world, whereupon he had removed his viola from under his chin, his face deathly pale, and was overwhelmed by one, all-consuming impulse.

'Alas, whither will fate take me . . .?' The singing voice faltered. Gasparo was embraced at length by the sobbing viola player.

Then the harpsichord fell silent. The orchestra wept. And so did the entire audience. An insight comparable to pain had overwhelmed the senses of the audience. Now there was room only for tears. Deaf and blind, sniffling pathetically, the audience seemed to have taken leave of their senses. The opposite was the case. In this electric air it suddenly dawned on every soul in the house what the commotion in London was all about.

The Virtuoso

There's history, and then there's the future, too. In between the two is the fascinating moment when the world changes. Tomorrow we will know more than today. The people of London naturally rated reason and irony far higher than bad taste and studied solemnity. In the mean time, however, they did everything they could to lure the Italian singers who had undergone testicular surgery to their opera houses. Ardent admiration. Adoration. Behind the lidded eyes the very latest truths – the twilight mastered, God restored to heaven – were relegated to the second plane. Progression: anyone who lifts a stone seldom stops to wonder where the scurrying black bugs manage to find shelter again, so incredibly quickly. The air in the Covent Garden theatre was filled with deep sighs because a miracle that was unlike anything on earth was to be without future. The virtuoso singer was worshipped with the senses. How else can one believe in God? Gasparo's beardless, arrogant beauty was a digression from the path of life, a history in the shade.

The embrace had lasted long enough. Gasparo disengaged himself. He took a step backwards and stared at Mr Christopher Swift with astonishment. He gave the violinist a pat on the shoulder and went over to the left of the stage. He stooped. His eyes sought out the composer who, his chin on his breast, sat and waited behind his lectern.

Shouldn't we get on with it?

At once the audience was refreshed by the blithe triple time of the duet in D major from the middle act. A second soprano emerged from the wings.

*

The future has yet to begin. I bring my face close to his. Gasparo has stopped talking at last, and that is just as well. I was on the point of getting a cramp. He, a man of twenty-eight, is ardently desired by a woman of twenty-seven, his words have made me pleasantly giddy, but right now I long for the smothered sounds of love. The fragrance of wood, a gently swaying ship's cabin, this is pure paradise. On my knees and resolute, I fumble with the sleeves of the already unbuttoned white shirt so as to slip them smoothly off his arms one by one. And those tight-fitting trousers must come off too.

VIII

Raise your hips. A deft movement of both my hands and a few tugs around the ankles result in an all-inclusive image: my stark-naked obsession in full glory. My glance slides innocently to his face. Apathy, inertia. That inertia is an intimate agreement between the two of us. What shall I do next to transmit my passion to you? When I take off my petticoat over my head, elbows raised, you can observe the gentle curve of my belly and my luxuriant black pubic hair, in my armpits you can discover beads of perspiration. A wrinkle forms above his nose. As if reaching out to a distant horizon, he stretches an arm towards me. Yes, I say warmly, please me. This is life. Why make yourself out to be so precious? The idol should be human, there is nothing more terrifying than pure heaven. I push my hair back and lean forward. We are practised lovers. Never mind that the circumstances have seen fit to endow my beloved with a singular, boyish member, ivory-white and sleepy, when my red mouth wraps itself around it, it will soon stretch out contentedly. Gentle envelopment. Deepest devotion. Shall we stay standing or shall we lie down? Shall we make light, rocking movements or shall we work towards a finale on the edge of madness while we sink our nails, our teeth, into tender flesh? Shall we kiss the French way or shall we touch our mouths only a little and leave them, as wrapped-up presents, for what they are? I see his eyes light up. I think our love has improved enormously since November. Sometimes it takes only a tiny signal on my part to arouse his interest. I scratch my ankle, he straightens his back. I lick the wine off my lips, he pushes his glass out of the way. The day will yet come when he shoves me up against the wall like any boatswain and lets himself go with broad, running strokes against my body, and I, for sure, will hitch up my skirts with pleasure. He takes my hand. I look at his close-set eyelashes. He grabs my wrists – he is on top of me already – and forces them up above my head. Deeply moved, I look at his velvety throat, his shoulders are softer and rounder than mine, God knows why, but beauty demands consolation and embracing. Our facial muscles slacken. With his belly pressed against mine I can feel his impatient nature, with his hands gripping my thighs I undergo his unashamed egoism. The light around us becomes coppery. When he enters me it is as if he is sinking to the ground before my feet with a measure of

devotion that, I believe, is not unlike the devotion of
those wretches you see in the Duomo hastily crossing
themselves in the dark, cool passage behind the altar,
the kind of supplicant who sets about invoking the
Virgin and the saints but who, still reeling from the
shock of coming from a sun-baked square into the
incense-filled stony gloom, loses all track of the sub-
stance of his pious entreaties and, after his 'Lord have
mercy,' his 'Holy Mary pray for me,' finds himself
engrossed in trivialities of money, vengeance, health,
only to succumb via a delirium of supplication, a chaos
of passionate outpourings, to a dubious cataleptic state
of wordless moaning, sighing, sobbing over the afternoon, the sun, a fly on your arm and the swell of the
sea.

*

Then the last night arrives. This was the final performance. The end of the season is announced in the San
Carlo theatre with a fanfare of trumpets. We all jump to
our feet and cheer not only the singers but also the
prompter and the fire-maker. 'Bravo! Bravissimo!' The
great finale of *Il Demetrio* is over. I join in the roar
unthinkingly. When the applause dies away at last, I go
to the dressing-room where Gasparo is exchanging his
royal costume for a suit of travelling clothes.

He takes off his wig and turns to me. His hair is
soaking wet.

'It's almost two,' he says. 'All being well the carriage will be waiting at the stage entrance by now.'

I nod. I know. D'Elbeuf, Gasparo's friend for life, has offered us the use of a carriage with four russet horses. We plan to cover the hundred and thirty miles to Rome in less than twenty hours.

A servant comes in to take our travelling bags.

'Take a drink before we go,' I say. 'Have you got everything?'

'Yes. Perhaps we'd better be off.'

Gasparo fumbles in his coat pockets, pulls out a sheet of paper and dons a black hat. As we turn left into the corridor we catch a glimpse, in a flood of noise, of the commotion on the stage and in the auditorium. The benches in the pit have been moved out of the way. We will not stay for the ball that will continue until daybreak, for tomorrow is Giuseppe's stage début in Rome.

It is pitch-dark outside. Yet we fly across the city, because we have two horsemen with torches racing ahead of our carriage. Past the city gate we are forced to slow down. The horses can jangle their harness bells for all they're worth, an ox-cart refuses to budge even an inch and also a table with four women playing cards by the light of a lamp remains standing.

At last we reach the road to Capua.

This is our last night, I think. I say: 'I wonder how that urchin will perform tomorrow.'

The Virtuoso

From the darkness he says drowsily: 'Quick. Pure. Incredibly agile in written-out acciaccaturas, hm, yes, I don't know if you've ever heard him sing *Mare crudele* . . .'

His voice fades. I can hear the bench across us creak, he stretches his legs. There is no sound but the rattle of wheels. Let me make myself comfortable too. Let me tuck my legs under me and rest my head against the upholstery to catch a few hours' sleep in this grinding gloom which is driving me back, yard by yard into my private history, the hollow in the earth where I cup my hands around a little flame and detach myself from most things, but not all.

His striped stockings, his white shirts, his cambric cravats in a variety of bright hues, it wasn't so much that he had a weakness for clothes, he simply took them seriously. Dressed in a suit of topaz velvet he studied his reflection gravely, put one foot forward and adjusted his cuffs. Vain, but by no means slow-witted. Crude. Generous. Stolid, yet strongly assertive. Waiting in the wings for his cue he would take a glass of muscatel wine and then, with calculating intensity, invoke the Virgin of Carmine. On one occasion, when a stage-hand moving a heavy piece of scenery accidentally jolted his back, his prayer turned without interruption into a flood of abuse as foul as a coachman's – that was not kind of him. His Neapolitan was surprisingly good, but there was a hint of an accent that grated on the ear like a pebble in your shoe. What is happiness? Four-hand symphonies on the cembalo. A meal and a single-minded conversation with a few painful dissonants. Four o'clock in the afternoon. Never will I stop thinking about his body. It smelled more delicious than the sea, it felt like air, it belonged, courtesy of my feverish love, to a far more explicit gender than the rest of mankind put together. Winter. Through the window of the bedroom we could see swallows nesting in the gables of the via San Carlo. I will remember Naples for ever as a city where the air is filled with the overtones of music and the murmurings of love. He was taciturn during that final week. When I offered him an amaretto and my lips, he accepted both with gratitude because he was in dire need of consolation. He had missed Giuseppe from the moment the boy left for Rome.

What is happiness, I think, and drop off to sleep.

Morning light. Barking dogs. The carriage has halted. We open our eyes to see where we are: on a track leading down from a stone cottage to a river, where an outsize barge is moored at a jetty made of boulders and planks. We have to cross the water.

Gasparo takes out his watch.

'Half past six,' he says.

I slip my feet into my shoes. 'I expect they'll have some food here, don't you?'

'I'm thirsty.'

'Me too. And I have to pee.'

'Goodness, yes!'

'Actually I slept quite well.'

'I had a very odd dream.'

'What about?'

The carriage door swings open. Our cheerful Sicilian driver wishes us good morning in a rush of air scented with trees and grass and then stoops to unfold the steps.

'Where are we?' I ask him.

'This is the Garigliano. The Appian Way starts on the other side.'

Threading our way among the thorny bushes to the cottage, we are preceded by the dogs. The creatures have stopped barking, they just turn now and then to stare at us dumbly.

'Would you like an omelette?' ask the ferryman's wife and daughter. 'Would you like coffee? We have crayfish, freshly caught. There's cheese, too.'

The small cottage smells of fire and iron. Through a door we glimpse a soot-covered wall and the tools of a smith, and through the window, framed by white gardenias, the river.

'Take off your shoes, and your stockings, too.'

Gasparo and I place our feet on the floor of stamped earth. The horses are being fed and watered. With the exception of the two horsemen, who will return to Naples from here, we all eat rather quickly. A final swig from the ladle and the driver and his mate set about manoeuvring the carriage and horses on to the barge, and soon we glide away, Gasparo and me, our feet rinsed clean, we stand at the railing and gaze at the reeds, an overhanging tree, a rocky path up a hillside dotted with sheep, a bend in the river, the horses are at rest, they will not be needed much longer as we are to catch the post-chaise in Gaeta. In the pale sky hovers a bird.

I point.

'A buzzard?' I wonder.

'An eagle?' Gasparo says, and, after a moment's pause: 'Just imagine, it's only two months since he turned up on my doorstep, in his jerkin and overcoat, and I knew at once that here was a good little fire and all it needed was some gentle and judicious poking. And how satisfying it was to help him in that short time to master a rapid *martellato* in the high register!'

His eyes scan my features. Perhaps he expects me to sympathize, but I do not react to the picture he conjures up for me: Giuseppe, a pallid, almost transparent, young man glancing quickly at his tutor before bursting forth with a mystery of head-notes in Ah! and Oh! I have grown quite fond of him. Wonderful, the admiration awaiting him in Rome, but I do not talk about him with Gasparo. Our shared winter, Gasparo, was made up of the theatre, of the town, of the days and the nights, I loved to hear your persistent monologues, and when I lay down beside you I felt your feats-in-arms slide down my belly. But with this new love you are treading your own familiar ground.

'It's going to be a warm day,' he says.

His hand rests on the railing, diamonds on three fingers. He had talked me into joining him on this trip the day before yesterday, when all I wanted was to blot out an unutterably sad dream I had had in the night. Why don't you keep me company? he had said. We could at least travel together. Didn't you say you had relatives in Rome?

I look up at the sky again. A bird. And as for the sun, it is shining straight into my face.

'Wait, I think I'd better put my hat on.'

Once we are on the far side of the river it takes less than an hour to reach Gaeta, where we change vehicles. Do give our regards to d'Elbeuf, we say as we clamber into a post-chaise. The driver knows full well that, after due payment, we expect to have covered a considerable distance by noon so that we can stop for refreshments in the land of popes. A fresh team of horses is harnessed and two demons of postilions take up their posts, with half-lowered hood we bowl along the high street, over a bridge, our pace slackens as we overtake a band of soldiers before turning into a straight road across lemon orchards in bloom, the whip cracks. Now and then the drivers twist their heads round and drum their chests triumphantly, shouting: 'What did I tell you, sir!' Or: 'Upon my honour!'

I fall silent. Blossom, dappled light pours in from all sides, beside me Gasparo is equally silent, what is there to be understood, gnarled trunks flit past in the grassy verge, a froth of white treetops whirls overhead. Can this be true, I think, I am leaving Naples. The winter is over. Together with Gasparo I leave the city with the Spanish palaces. The horses with the Moorish saddle-cloths. Each day I used to ride under an arch of Catalonian design and then past a school. Whenever the windows were open I would hear the children reciting their lessons in chorus. Chained to an almond tree in the yard there was a brightly coloured bird, which would sway from side to side to Virgil's metrical beat, on some days it would sing loudly along with the children. Throughout the entire winter I succeeded in keeping my mind blank and yet not losing it.

But by the time Velletri looms in the distance, I can no longer think straight. However, we still took some food in Sezze, where we still changed the one team of horses for another, in a roadside chapel that served as a tavern we still drank chilled Samos wine among brambles and ferns, but on the steep road to Velletri I became sad. I had dozed off, my cheek resting on my fist. I woke with a start and fixed my eyes on him. He grinned sheepishly. I looked out of the window. Where are we? When he said: I think this must be near Velletri, my pulse began to quicken. It's all very well for you to yawn, I think. It's all very well to smirk like an imbecile! Isn't it nice to be travelling so peacefully together? An olive grove here, a sprinkling of cows there, why think ahead to Rome, to the tollgate where our ways will part for ever? And you know as well as I do that there are always coaches for hire at the Tor di Mezzavia. One will be found to take me to the house of Don Grigio, Berto's first cousin, while another transports you directly to the *palazzo* in the purple neighbourhood, where not only Giuseppe but also his illustrious tutor are to be the guests of Cardinal Aldobrandini. My lips tremble. The road climbs. It seems to me that a mist is falling. Velletri is reputed to be a pretty town on a hill, but at this rate we will not see much of it.

'It's getting very misty,' my eternal love informs me.

I bite my lip. I do not reply. Our chaise, with half-lowered hood, rides into a cloud. The mist thickens rapidly until even the two drivers disappear before our very eyes. Yes, go! I think. I forgive you. Forget about our afternoons, our *coitus sublimatus*. Forget the reversed Venus. I will forgive you when you lie in the arms of I care not whom and forget the deep butterfly stroke of which, after so much cosseting on my part, you have grown inordinately fond. Forget the cadence that you can only have with a woman, forget if you must!

Thick fog. There is nothing to be seen. Even Gasparo has vanished. 'Gasparo!' I still cry weakly. No response, only a few chill droplets on my face. Overcome by death-like solitude, I wring my hands. Curves, loops, the horror of light that is utterly opaque, I can feel we are twisting upwards with only a hand's breadth between us and an icy void. My mind is wandering.

Then I become aware of a virtual standstill.

How long have I been absent? I do not know. There was no space. There was nothing but a clammy atmosphere in which it was unthinkable even to stir a finger. I am too dazed to speak. Ahead of me I feel the colossal power of the horses. We reach the crest of the hill, and begin the descent. A light breeze blows the world back to us.

Warmth. Space.

'Goodness me . . .' murmurs Gasparo. He gives me a quizzical look. For a moment I think I can see my own bewilderment in his eyes. '. . . and then in ten days or so off to Vienna.' His hair is as wet as at the end of a performance.

He shifts about on his seat. 'Actually I'm quite looking forward to it.'

Oh sweet Jesus, Holy Mary, I forgive you from the bottom of my heart! My blood begins to course again. All right then, go! Take a carriage to Vienna, to Dresden, take a ship to London and demand staggering fees. Demand sumptuous apartments. Demand servants. Always insist on singing one more aria than anyone else and be as truculent as you can. No one can outshine you, remember that. Remember how much effort must be expended before beauty can embrace lust and luxuriance. Let them all fawn on you, just store away my face and my name in a slumbering corner of your soul. Make your entrances in your customary off-hand manner against a background of statues or Syrian gardens (they think up the most exotic settings these days), feel free to encapsulate my person and our love-making, quite ingenuously, in a highly ornamented aria.

'What is it?' he asks. 'What are you smiling at?'

But I shake my head. We have been travelling for the past twenty-four hours. The Lord knows how tired I am. 'What about Vienna, what will you sing there?' I mutter, my swollen eyes fixed on meadows, hillsides, a vineyard that reminds me of long ago.

'. . . an old Cavalli opera, the *Serse* I believe, but as you know . . .'

Under a thatched shelter, a farm girl lies asleep, a dog at her feet.

'. . . they wrote me a letter . . . they know what I'm like . . .'

The fields are deserted at this time of day. Now and then we come across a solitary cart. The farmhouses to one side have all their weather-beaten shutters closed. Little boys splash about in a pool fringed with white gravel.

'In the summers,' Gasparo says after a silence, 'we would go to the Savio gorge, there would still be water there even in August.'

'I know,' I say, 'you walked there in the shade of a row of plane trees.'

'We used to shout across the gorge to hear the echo.'

'I know,' I repeat. 'Sometimes all you needed to do was open your mouth and the sound would come back to you.'

'True. But when the sun was high in the sky it could also happen that your cry was met by silence, a silence that lasted until you'd forgotten you were still waiting, your chin on your knees. When the echo came at last you'd keel over from the shock.'

'Your father owned one of the vineyards close by.'

'So he did. When it rained while the sun was out he'd insist you could already smell the *rosso*.'

'The houses in the village were painted a light shade of red.'

'They pounded iron from dawn to dusk in La Pina's workshop.'

'By the side of the road to Campetiello there used to be smoke rising from the ground.'

'On summer nights we would climb up the volcano until we could hear the crackle of the leaping flames.'

'I would have loved to hear that sound, but Faustina wouldn't let me go up there.'

The chaise grinds to a halt. The postilions, having felt the dry wind on their faces, realize that we will now have the sun straight in front of us. They jump to the ground, raise the hood fully and secure it with clamps. Suddenly Gasparo and I find ourselves in an upholstered twilight.

The Virtuoso

'So you heard me sing as a boy,' he says.

'Yes, I used to screw up my eyes with delight.'

We look at blurred visions bathed in the warm late-afternoon sun. The Appian Way takes us inexorably to our destination. Our separation draws near to the accompaniment of ever-thickening traffic on the thoroughfare. We see wagons with Greeks, Syrians, fattened roosters, a stack of slippery logs is lashed tight by a ragged-looking fellow and a girl of striking agility.

Between us hangs a fatigue verging on delirium. 'Did you see that magnificent horse?' we say, and: 'I'm not very fond of icaco bushes.' 'I quite agree.' At one point Gasparo murmurs: 'I wish you all the best,' whereupon I reply: 'I feel I'm losing my mind.'

Then we arrive at a certain old stone terminus known as Tor di Mezzavia. Having alighted and paid for our fare, we make our way through the jostling crowd of people and horses to the door of the inn. Since it doesn't escape me that Gasparo, without so much as a glance, is about to walk out of my life, I step across the threshold to block his path. A crowd gathers on either side of the narrow entrance.

He looks at me in wonderment.

'Put your arms around me,' I say.

He gestures vaguely.

'Both of them.'